Faith and a Fast Gun

Riding into trouble was a habit with ex-Pinkerton detective Joshua Dillard and his sentimental journey to a mission graveyard in Texas proved no exception. Guns blazed and chips flew off the headstones as he intervened to save a girl called Faith from the clutches of Lyte Grumman and his gunhawks.

Joshua learned that Grumman was a ruthless cattle baron who'd lost a thousand head of longhorns in what he reckoned was a rigged poker game. Grumman was intent on recouping his loss, whatever it took. . . .

Buying in on Faith's behalf, Joshua soon found his skills with a Colt Peacemaker to no avail against superior numbers and a deadly tangle of inopportune passions and double-cross.

Then a grim past and a frightful present turned Faith's hand insanely against all men!

Faith and a Fast Gun

Chap O'Keefe

A Black Horse Western

ROBERT HALE · LONDON

© Chap O'Keefe 2010
First published in Great Britain 2010

ISBN 978-0-7090-8854-7

Robert Hale Limited
Clerkenwell House
Clerkenwell Green
London EC1R 0HT

www.halebooks.com

Typeset by
Derek Doyle & Associates, Shaw Heath
Printed and bound in Great Britain by
CPI Antony Rowe, Chippenham and Eastbourne

1

GIRL IN A GRAVEYARD

She left the general store and saw them across the dust-filled ruts of the main street, lounging on the porch under the faded sign that said BLACK JACK SALOON: cattleman Lyte Grumman, his mooncalf son Chet and two of their rough ranch-hands.

All warmth seemed to drain from her cheeks. For a moment she just gaped. They were the very last people she wanted to see in Ciudad del Rio.

It had been a mistake to come into town, since, until now, the bunch had likely assumed she'd vamoosed many weeks ago with Dick, who'd taken off Grumman a worthwhile chunk of his Slash C herd – a thousand head of Texas longhorns. A note for the cattle had been put on the table after Grumman had run out of chips at poker in the gaming parlour above the Black Jack's bar-room.

She clasped to the silken curves of her bosom the latest Eastern ladies' journals she'd been tempted to come into town to collect – these now oh-so dangerously alluring purchases with pictures of the fall fashions – and averted her face.

She tripped hurriedly, head down, along the plank walk in her shiny, shell-cordovan shoes with the rounded toes, metal eyelets and inch-and-a-half heels. But it was too late.

'Hey!' a voice exclaimed. 'Ain't that the smart bitch who was in cahoots with Redvers?'

She didn't look back but could see the accusing, pointing finger in her mind's eye. She heard the swift mumble of oaths and confirmations, the shuffling motion of heavy feet that preceded a shift into pursuit.

'Miss Faith!' they called after her.

One request came in the familiarly beseeching tones of Chet Grumman. 'Faith – wait!'

Lyte Grumman himself joined the baying of his hounds – growly, dictatorial.

'Hold up, damn you, missy! We want words.'

Tucking the Eastern papers under her arm, Faith lifted her full skirt clear of her trim ankles, showing the lacy edge of a fine white petticoat, and broke into a run. She skipped off the end of the plank walk and kept right on going.

Her nimbleness and abandon of decorum availed her little.

The heavy-footed Slash C pack, led by its boss,

Grumman, pounded closer.

On the town's boundary was its oldest building, an adobe mission church completed in the 1770s, more than a hundred years before. She swung into its grounds blindly, between open wrought-iron gates under an ornate archway in lime-washed walls.

To the left was a sunbaked graveyard, a proliferation of mounds, markers and jumbled headstones, some older even than the church, severely weathered, leaning and crumbling. She darted behind one of the newer stones with its inscription still legible: THOMAS D. HARTNETT. Born 5 Jan 1834. Died 23 Mar 1877.

Her breath was coming now in short gasps, the result of exertion, fright, or both.

But running and hiding got her nowhere at all. The cemetery was no sanctuary. Grumman's men quickly spotted and came after her at their ease. She shrank back.

'You don't have any call to bother me!' she cried. 'Keep away from me!'

One of the Slash C riders, Kurt Schwimmer, a big bulky man with mean eyes and a grim mouth, approached purposefully and fastened a hard hand on her shoulder.

'Gal, you got some tellin' to do!'

She felt huge revulsion at his touch.

'L-leave me be! Go away! G-get out of here!' she stammered.

Chet Grumman came up, his eyes shining and his loose, full lips wet. He was a slimly built young man, a mite above average height, fair-haired and with swanky style that showed weakness of character and, Faith suspected, was also a mask for a streak of viciousness.

'Faith, my pretty,' he said, 'Pa doesn't want to – uh – make trouble for you, but it's crazy to deny him what he wants to know. He figures to get back the dinero owing for his beeves.'

She bit her lip. She wasn't Chet's 'pretty'. She'd made that perfectly obvious on past, less uncivilized occasions when he'd pressed his suit. But he was plainly still crazy about her – correction, about wanting to have relations with her – and it gave her one small advantage to play on.

'Chet, I can't help your father,' she said, sighing. 'I don't know where Dick is. Maybe I could let you persuade me not to care where he is. . . .'

But it was difficult to infuse her change of tune with any conviction. It would take a different kind of woman in a different place to achieve the intended, subtle air of challenging suggestion. And the simple fact was that any thought of male attention, let alone under circumstances like these, filled her with panic.

It always did; it was how she was.

Lyte Grumman lumbered up. His cruel laugh was a blood-chilling sound. He had skin the texture and colour of an old potato and his muddy eyes were cold and unwinking.

'We got you hard and fast, bitch! You'll do some singing. No one to hear 'cept us and the dead! No one to stop us—'

That was when, the panic rising, she yanked free of Schwimmer's grasp, ripping the shoulder of her dress. She tried to throw herself past Grumman and his son, and when Grumman grabbed hold of her, she struck at his face with long, neatly manicured nails. She brought up a knee.

But Grumman laughed again and turned a tree-trunk thigh to absorb what might have been a painful, crippling blow. He was a powerful man and held her effortlessly.

Sobbing with fury and horror, she squirmed under his hands. 'Stop detaining me!'

Chet said excitedly, 'Honey, you'll get yourself hurt!'

Grumman said, 'Hell, she's a wildcat!'

Schwimmer said, 'No never-mind, Chet's lovin' watchin' it. He likes a gal with some spirit. Jest means thar'll be fun gettin' her to spill what she knows!'

Chet's eyes were indeed gleaming.

Hotly, Faith fought, her hair coming unpinned and spilling to her shoulders. But Grumman dragged her further into the extensive burial ground, away from the church and the road.

'No knowing what can happen to a gal who gets lost in a graveyard,' he mocked. 'But mebbe we won't do it here. Better go get the buckboard, Nolan, and bring it round the back boundary. We'll take her along with us.'

Chet put clammy hands on her to help his father, and Schwimmer trailed along behind.

Faith started to scream.

San Antonio had grown since Joshua Dillard had last visited. He had come by train and stagecoach nigh on 900 miles from Denver to find the South-western city prospering as a cattle, distribution, mercantile and military centre serving the Border region and the South-west.

Its population had swelled, they said, to 20,000. It was the southern hub and supplier of the cattle trail drives; an important wool market had developed with the importation of merino sheep to the adjacent Hill Country.

Yet to Joshua it was still the hard, unlovely place where, as an operative of the famous Allan Pinkerton Detective Agency, he'd learned that thief-taking and wife-taking didn't mix.

It was in this town, on one day of sickening bloodshed years before, that the Wilder gang had come calling on the home he'd provided for a sparkling-eyed, peachy-cheeked bride with spun-gold hair. The outlaws, full of malice toward a 'Pink', had done more than wreck the place. They'd snuffed out the warming flame of his wife's beautiful young life and forever changed the course of his own.

The loss had turned his heart to stone.

Obsessed with a hatred of lawbreakers which inclined him to irrationality and illegality in his actions, he'd been obliged to resign his Pinkerton job less he should embarrass the agency.

In the cold, lonely years that followed, he'd grown

lean and very hard from an assortment of shrewdly chosen labours as a freelance troubleshooter. Most of these had ended in blood and turmoil, yet never quite his own death. And seldom with financial reward.

Thus the recent Bennett case in Colorado had proved an exception. A grateful mining millionaire had pressed a handsome sum of money on Joshua for saving him, his wife and his sister from an insane outlaw's revenge.

Joshua had decided to take the unusual opportunity to visit his wife's grave and indulge, for once, in the poignant memories he would never completely shrug off.

It was summertime and the mercury in the thermometer at the renowned Menger Hotel, a two-floor cut-stone building which featured an abundance of classical detail, was nudging the hundred-degrees mark. San Antonio, Joshua remembered, was hot and alternately dry or humid depending on prevailing winds. And the cuisine offered in the hotel's Colonial Dining Room included mango ice-cream, among other tempting specialities like wild game and snapper soup made from turtles caught in the San Antonio River.

But Joshua dallied less than a day sampling the Menger luxuries, albeit the hotel had the reputation of being the finest west of the Mississippi. The morning after his arrival in the city, he went early to a livery established by another German immigrant on South Alamo Street. Here, he dickered for a big

11

sorrel mare to carry him the last forty-odd miles of his journey of remembrance.

The grave of his wife was in the cemetery of the mission at Ciudad del Rio, the small town which had been her birthplace.

The sorrel had the stamina and the reaching stride to eat up the miles without churning a rider's mid-section. Ciudad del Rio was reached in the late afternoon, after resting up in the shade of an oak grove around midday when the heat was at its peak. Joshua felt well satisfied with his bargain purchase of the horse.

Ciudad del Rio was no San Antonio but it was a thriving cattle town and ranching centre in its own right, a sprawl of board and adobe. It offered most of the usual conveniences. The essential commercial premises, including a bank, a hotel, a livery barn, a big general store and a saloon, the Black Jack, were on the main street or bordering a wide plaza where the buildings had thick adobe walls, mostly lime-washed. Down the several cross streets, Joshua glimpsed the weathered buildings of a feed barn, a bakery, a small café, a barber shop and a dressmaker's.

He didn't waste any time in town but hied himself to the old mission grounds and the sprawling cemetery, not suspecting that events there would take a swift, unexpected turn.

He left the sorrel tied at the gate. The burial ground, even in the last of the warm daylight, was forlorn and bleak as such places are inclined to be.

12

He picked his way through the tombs, the headstones; the cheaper, wooden markers with crude, pokerwork inscriptions; the mounds marked and unmarked, weed-grown or carefully maintained.

By a quirk of history or design of the mission's long departed founders, the older parts of the graveyard were situated furthest from the church and the road. His wife's family had been among the earliest Anglo-American arrivals, and it was in this remote section that he relocated her headstone.

A few of the nearby graves had flowers; others had mussel shells and stones from the local creek as decoration. His wife's grave was unadorned. Its rock headstone was already covered with spots of lichen and a thin growth of moss.

Joshua was contemplating how he might remedy this dereliction brought about by the almost drifting pattern of his life throughout the Frontier West when, bursting upon his thoughts, came the violent interruption of a woman's screams.

His immediate thoughts condemned the disrespect such a racket showed to a hallowed place. An angry oath formed on his lips. Who had the right to bring squalid conflicts here? He supposed, reasonably enough, that some assignation in the privacy of the graveyard hadn't panned out quite how the female player had wanted. She'd changed her mind maybe, prompting a cheated swain into rough assertion of his demands.

But Joshua's cuss words died before they could be uttered.

A party of four lurched into his sight between the graves and the untrimmed junipers that had been allowed to take a dense hold in the far-flung reaches of the burial ground. Joshua saw one woman, dressed like a lady but dishevelled, and three men in range garb. Two of the men had hold of the woman. Her screams were more distress than indignation.

The odds in the uneven struggle were more than Joshua could stomach. A man with his history lived by a code. At his innocent wife's graveside, the inner voice of it spoke especially loud.

'Save me!' the girl cried, providing the last straw.

'Hold up, you sons of bitches!' Joshua roared.

'Hell, who are you, mister?' the man behind said. 'Keep your sticky beak outa Mr Grumman's business!'

He also went to draw a gun from his belt holster.

Joshua beat him to it. He dragged out a .45 Colt Peacemaker of his own. The gun was well worn and scarred by a crack in the blackened right grip, but it was in top working order.

Its bark was followed by a scream from the foolhardy aggressor, who was thrown heavily against a tombstone, dropping his weapon. His right arm dangled and blood spilled quickly from a spreading crimson blotch on his sleeve to drip from his fingers into the dust.

Swearing, the men holding the girl reacted by pure instinct. They let her go and grabbed for their guns.

'Run!' Joshua yelled to the frightened girl. 'Get

out of the way!'

Joshua himself lunged for the cover of his wife's headstone. Lead whined off the side of it, scattering rock chips and grey dust. He came up on to one knee, sighted swiftly over its top and squeezed trigger again.

The shot went close and the men who'd held the girl – one about fifty, the other in his twenties – scattered in different directions.

Joshua wasn't looking for a fight. He also took the chance to run, starting back toward the church, the road and his new sorrel horse – the direction taken by the girl.

But it was then that a fourth man came on the scene, shouting at the fleeing pair, asking what in the devil's name was going on and where did they want the goddamned buckboard now.

'The bastard winged Kurt. Stop him, Nolan!' rapped the older, heavy-set man who was presumably 'Mr Grumman'.

Not knowing what he was stumbling into, Nolan had broken four-square into the open. Seeing Joshua, he, too, belatedly palmed up his six-gun, pointing the muzzle toward the stranger.

Joshua's Peacemaker thundered. Flame, smoke and lead spewed from the barrel. The impact of the .45 slug sent Nolan reeling. He tripped on the kerbstone of a grave and went down across its covering of sharp-edged shells with a shriek.

Triumphant but mightily puzzled, Joshua streaked for the gates. By the time Grumman and the younger man gave chase, he was beyond effective pistol-shot range, though it bothered him when he caught up with the girl his intervention had saved.

She was hovering inside the mission grounds, either out of uncertainty about where she should head, or to see what had become of her rescuer.

He felt frustrated. 'I just gave you a chance to get away. Do you want them to catch you again?'

She shook her head vigorously. 'No – oh heavens, no! I'm full of gratitude. Lyte and Chet Grumman will have no mercy. But what should I do?'

He turned, revolver poised, and it pleased him to see Grumman and the younger man – a son maybe? – check, fearful as they came close to within range. He made a rapid decision.

'We'll have to go double,' he told the girl, nodding toward the patient sorrel hitched at the gates. 'Are you willing to ride astride?'

She looked apprehensively at the big horse and swallowed.

'I'm not a farm sort of girl,' she said, 'but I'll try anything to escape those brutes.'

She had enough familiarity with what was expected to reach up for the saddle horn and cantle and put a neatly shoed left foot into the stirrup.

Joshua place his hands on her hips to give a helping, hurrying lift. She seemed to flinch some at his touch, as though she found it distasteful. The expensive, silky stuff of her dress slipped on the layers of what was beneath and Joshua held the harder, acutely aware of the shape and firmness of the outer bones of her pelvis.

'Oh, my! Ohh. . . !'

She gave a further gasp and swung her right leg frantically over the saddle. Despite the urgency of the moment, Joshua observed it was a very graceful leg, well proportioned and shaped. Seated, but still unable to settle safely in the saddle, she was obliged to hike her skirts above the knee, uncovering ankles and calves and affording fleeting glimpses of more.

Joshua sensed her displeasure and saw the fire on her cheeks, but then he was unhitching the sorrel and flinging himself up on to the cantle behind her. He reached around her for the reins, coming into contact with a stiff back and firm buttocks.

Grumman was bellowing at them to stop. Any moment, Joshua expected to feel the wind, and possibly the paralysing impact, of a bullet. But fortunately, it seemed the girl was of value to them alive, not dead, and no shots came.

He dug his heels into the sorrel's sides and plunged the horse, untroubled by the double burden, into headlong flight. The landmark of the church, with its red-shingled roof and shimmering white bell-tower, quickly couldn't be seen for the dust behind them.

'Relax and lean back or we'll spill!' Joshua commanded his unhappy companion.

The wind whipped the girl's trailing hair about his face. Like it or not, she became nestled against him, hotness and softness and roundness pressed close between the muscular hardness of his thighs. He felt the thunder of her heartbeats.

What, Joshua wondered, have I gotten myself into this time?

2

HOUSE OF DESPAIR

'Are you sure this is the right place?'

'Of course I'm sure. I know where I live!'

If houses had faces, this one's was the face of a drunk old hobo, wrinkled and sagging. Dirty. Its windows might have been the blank eyes of a blind man.

It was a half-hour's walk from the centre of Ciudad del Rio, but it was a walk few ever cared to make. They had ridden here circuitously on the back of the big sorrel, throwing off any reasonable possibility of pursuit and finally descending by a weed-choked trail into a hollow around the turbid backwater of a creek.

Joshua couldn't believe that his ruffled but once smartly attired companion was claiming a dilapidated, two-storey frame house on the dark backwater's muddy bank as her home.

It was situated in the shadows of a small wood of mossy, distorted trees; bottomland hardwoods –

pecan, oak, cottonwood and hackberry – beneath which lay the trunks of specimens flung down by old hurricanes or storms. Broad-leaved shrubs growing around the tangle of debris bore what looked like black splotches of disease.

'I live here with my mother,' the girl said. 'We fell on hard times.'

Joshua slapped at a hungry mosquito which had left one of the many swarms of the whining critters to alight on the back of his left hand.

'And we are?' he probed.

'I'm Faith – Hartnett.'

'Hartnett. . . .' Joshua repeated, musing, trying to place where he'd recently seen the name.

'Yes. *Hartnett.* Thomas Hartnett – that's my father – was killed in a range war with Lyte Grumman. But do come in, please. I'm much indebted to you, Mr—?'

'Dillard, Joshua Dillard.'

'Well, Mr Dillard, you must meet my mother and tell us something about yourself. I've a hunch you could be just the man we need. . . .'

Intrigued, Joshua followed Faith into the forbidding, run-down house. Only stray beams of sunlight pierced the thicket to relieve its gloom.

'Mother!' Faith called. 'We have a visitor. In fact, more than a visitor – a good knight who rescued me from the foul hands of Grumman and his gunhawks.'

A wheezy voice responded in querulous alarm.

'*Grumman*! I warned you, Faith! You were a fool to show yourself in town. That Chet is still crazy about you, and old Lyte will never forgive you your part in the loss of his longhorns.'

'Oh, shush . . . I want to introduce you to Mr Dillard, Mother.'

Faith steered Joshua to a dowdy and cluttered front parlour within thin, clapboard walls where a seemingly aged woman sat in a rocking-chair.

To Joshua's further surprise, the mother was inclined to grossness, with a roundish, flabby-jowled face and distinctly multiple chins. Even in the poor light, Joshua discerned a shadow of moustache on her top lip. She was wrapped in an old red flannel dressing-gown which accentuated the size and shapelessness her daughter didn't share.

The contrast between the two women was out of the common run, but such were the tricks sometimes played by age and heredity.

'Mother, Mr Joshua Dillard,' Faith said formally; then, loud and firm as though her mother might be a little deaf or of feeble mind, 'Mr Dillard, Mrs Belle Hartnett.'

The eyes looked small in the mother's moon of a face, but Joshua detected a flicker of alertness in them. Training and a comprehensive experience of life told him Belle Hartnett was in fact an intelligent woman, maybe shrewd.

'Hmm!' she grunted to no consequence. 'Most interesting.'

'I think Mr Dillard deserves to hear our story, Mother,' Faith said.

'Do tell the han'some feller whatever you see fit, dearie. I leave the talking to you.'

21

Belle followed her advice with a laugh cut short by a fit of wheezy coughing which she stifled in a man-sized handkerchief.

Faith frowned, but began her harrowing tale.

'Lyte Grumman is boss not only of the Slash C cattle ranch, which is the biggest in this country, he now virtually rules the town of Ciudad del Rio and its environs. And the Slash C wasn't big enough for him. He was out to hog the whole country. He had to eliminate all the smaller outfits, like Tom Hartnett's.'

'Your father's,' Joshua said for clarification. 'Yours.'

'That's right. It's why we're hidden away here, isn't it, Mother?'

Belle gave a nod and a wheezy chuckle.

Faith went on, 'Some of the modest ranchers got tired of the fight and the grudges it caused. Some sold out; some got loans at the bank and were foreclosed at Grumman's instigation. The Slash C bought up the properties at the sheriff's sales.'

In his line of range-detective and troubleshooting business, Joshua had encountered similar situations.

'The old, old cattle-range story of greed – the lust for power.'

'Quite. Tom Hartnett – my father – held out, standing in the way of Grumman's ambitions. Trouble came thick and fast. The quarrelling frightened us. Boundaries were questioned, grazing and water rights challenged. Men died in silly, trumped-up disputes that steadily escalated the conflict. To cut a long story short, it became no less

22

than a full-scale range war. Grumman hired a tough crew. He still has more gun-hands on his payroll than ranch-hands. We were sick with fear and washed up long before Father was shot dead after going out alone to mend a deliberately broken drift fence.'

'Murder!' Joshua said. 'Was nothing done about it?'

Faith shrugged.

'What could be? The law in Ciudad del Rio is Grumman's law and there were no witnesses to what happened, no evidence. It wasn't for anyone to say Grumman had ordered his killing.'

Belle made a low moaning sound that could have been of despair, or just a hum of incredulous disapproval.

Joshua said, 'That stinks to high heaven. You must have been very bitter.'

'Maybe, but it was a kind of relief, too – to abandon the struggle, give up the spread, get out. The squeeze and the warring had left the Hartnetts hopelessly in debt.'

'You quit?'

Faith reflected a moment. 'Yes, we had to. Grumman had us over a barrel. But I haven't told you yet about Dick.'

'Who's Dick?'

'He's my brother.'

Her mother spluttered, burying her moon-like face in the handkerchief again.

'Is Mrs Hartnett all right?' Joshua asked. 'She must

find this – uh – raking over of the coals very upsetting.'

Faith let the attempted solicitude ride.

'We pin our hopes on Dick, but we seem to have lost him. It's why Grumman and his ruffians were after me. They think I know exactly where he is, but I don't and I wish I did – and not so I can tell them!'

Joshua noted her vehemence.

'Your brother ran out on you? Why did this happen? Surely, you and your mother needed him.'

Faith tried to smile. 'I'm sorry. I didn't intend to create the notion he deserted us. Dick had a plan to restore our fortunes. It hung on the fact that he's the smartest card player in the whole wide world.'

Now it was Joshua's turn to have trouble with a smile . . . in suppressing one. The son of a small-time South-west Texas rancher could be clever at cards, of course, but he wouldn't be in the same league as the professionals Joshua had known. His sister, who clearly thought a heap of his abilities, was letting family pride get in the way of judgement, even sense.

She said, 'Lyte Grumman has a weakness for gambling; also for strong whiskey, which he calls wild mare's milk.'

'Ah . . .' Joshua said, 'a fool combination.'

'I agree, Mr Dillard, and so did Dick. He said he'd make a sucker of Grumman, and being a right good poker player he did. In a long session in the private card room above the saloon, he plumb cleaned out Grumman of chips and all the ready money he had on him. Grumman being a man of local influence,

24

he could have used his name alone as security for more chips at the Black Jack anytime, but he'd drunk way too much and was his usual braggart self, full of pride. Dick was smart. He told him so many head of his herd would be enough for him to stay and raise!'

'And Grumman fell for it?'

'He knew Dick had put all he had in the pot and didn't think the breaks could keep going his way. Grumman bragged that no game in Ciudad del Rio was too rich for him. Maliciously, he figured luck had to change sometime in an all-night session and he'd have the fun of reducing to complete ruin the son of a rival who'd caused huge bother. In truth, the whole Hartnett family, meaning Ma and me, too, could be finished – done – on a turn of the cards. It really needs to be told here that I'd already upset Grumman's spoiled son Chet by rejecting his advances.'

Joshua tutted. 'Oh, what a tangled web!'

'Isn't it? Chet is arrogant and odious, and struts around like a bantam rooster. He believes he has a right to any woman in town he fancies, no strings attached. It's all disgustingly sordid. But that's another story. . . .'

'All right. Maybe for now you should go on with what happened in the poker game.'

'Well, Grumman's assumption Dick would be wiped out proved wrong. Dick never lost a hand. The chips and notes just piled up in front of him. Grumman seemed to be the biggest of losers. He tossed away useless hands with snarls and vulgar cusses. He drank more than his fill.

'When he finally found he could lay down two pair, kings and aces, he was beside himself at the thought of victory. He wrote another note for cattle, and a thousand head of his herd was now in the pot. But Dick pushed in his chips and called him! You see, he had three of a kind which beat Grumman's two pair.'

'Phew! Supposing Grumman had held four of a kind?'

Faith said, almost smugly, 'But he didn't, and Dick *knew.*'

Joshua shook his head wonderingly. 'Some coup. Very skilled, your brother. But where is he now, and where is all that wealth of cattle he won?'

'Ma and I put no trust in the local law, because it's in Grumman's pocket. We could have hired hands to run the cattle on what was left of our old graze, but the Slash C gunnies would never have allowed it – would they, Mother?'

Belle Hartnett wheezed and cackled. 'No! No! I do declare you tell it well, Faith.'

'So with misfortune sure to dog us here, and Grumman quickly accusing Dick of having cheated in the marathon poker session, we decided on an adventurous step. Dick would hire a trail boss and crew and drive the herd north to Montana. The plan was to set up there and start over, free from the feuding with the Grummans.'

Joshua nodded thoughtfully, tugging his lower lip. 'Sounds reasonable. Others have done it, and done well.'

Faith grimaced at him, but her mouth quivered when she opened it to resume the story.

'It has worked for some, I know, but whether it will for us, we don't know. Dick was supposed to have sent for Mother and me as soon as he found a place in Montana. But many weeks have gone by and we've heard nothing. . . .'

Joshua understood. 'Mighty worrying for you.'

'It is.'

'And the Grummans are plainly plumb bad medicine to cross. Is it safe for you to stay here? A defenceless woman with – no disrespect intended – just her mother for help?'

Faith sighed. 'You identify our predicament exactly, Mr Dillard. If it's not already evident to a man of sharp wits such as yourself, I must say that an argument has been in progress between Mother and myself about what we should do. Lyte Grumman hates to lose at anything. Maybe he has had Dick tracked and somehow scotched his intentions in Montana. We will never know unless I can go there – find Dick and determine what has happened.'

Belle about exploded into her handkerchief.

'Find Dick! Find Dick!' she gasped breathlessly as though she was astounded at the temerity of the proposal.

Joshua approached the problem logically, weighing the given facts.

'If Grumman knows where Dick and his herd are, what does he want with you?'

Faith shook her head sadly. 'I couldn't say. Perhaps

27

it's Chet's idea of sport. . . .'

'Damnit – beg pardon, ma'am and miss – we should have this out with the Grummans!'

'It would only lead to more trouble for yourself, Mr Dillard,' Faith said, concern strong in her voice. 'I've seen you're a . . . a . . . *fast gun*, but it doesn't do to buck the Grumman bunch hereabouts. Tom Hartnett was only one of many who have learned that.'

Joshua spread his hands. 'So what do you propose?'

'That I should leave for Montana forthwith. It will be less dangerous to quit Grumman's territory altogether and find out what has become of Dick.'

Belle rocked in her chair in an agitation that might have been tears or mirth. 'Dick! Dick! Can she do it?'

Faith looked at her crossly. 'Of course I can, Mother. I appreciate it's something a young woman would be much tested to accomplish on her own, perilous – but I have a new idea.'

'Oh. . . ?' Joshua said.

'Yes, I've a proposition. I will need a good, capable man to escort me. A fast gun. I believe I've found him!'

Fatalistically, Joshua saw his intervention in Faith's affairs was spiralling rapidly out of his control.

'You have?'

She ignored him and addressed Belle. 'We must agree that a percentage of Dick's winnings is to be realized and paid to Mr Dillard for his help. We will find Dick and order him so!'

'Oh, girl, you are a one!' the fat woman said.

Joshua was only tolerably peeved. Such troubleshooting was his job . . . but did he want the assignment Faith was in effect assuming he would accept? He was trapped, yet nicely so.

He would purely hate to get mixed into any range war, though he'd let it happen to him before and this time he wasn't in truth being asked to do exactly that.

Faith's pretty face was a picture of determination striving to overcome distress, framed by the tumbled disorder of her blonde hair. A wave of pity swept over him. It wasn't incumbent on him to horn into the mess . . . but, hell, he knew he would!

3

SLASH C HITS BACK

Joshua touched his heels to the ribs of the sorrel mare and cleared the trees that bordered the malodorous still water in the hollow's bottom. He rode up to the road and slowly back into town on the tired horse, unsure what he'd been let in for and silently taking himself to task over it.

He'd been inveigled into volunteering his services as a bodyguard and travelling companion with only dubious likelihood of reward at the end of the task, if indeed it could be brought to an outcome.

Thanks be that he still had much of grateful millionaire Ryan Bennett's donation to tide him over!

Still, on the plus side, and with dinero to chink unusually in his pockets, he could think of far worse ways of spending his time than riding trains and coaches the length of the land alongside an attractive young woman who, despite impoverished circumstances, managed to attire herself stunningly in clothes copied out of the latest smart papers from back East.

He had an admiration for this Faith Hartnett's courage, and he didn't think he was letting his head be turned by the obvious appeal of a beautiful, poised and unattached woman.

He'd seen at first hand that Miss Faith and Mrs Belle Hartnett were in a hole in more ways than one. Gallantry alone had demanded he give consideration to Faith's case. And now he was committed – enlisted with the task of organizing his and her departure at the earliest date.

'Grumman's men are on to me and will never let me leave Ciudad del Rio alone,' Faith had told him. 'You must buy two tickets and be with me when I ride the stage out.'

Joshua sat easily in the saddle and let the horse pick a steady gait of her own.

He fell to thinking about the missing brother and his desperate undertaking in driving a herd of a thousand Texas longhorns up the Western Trail, past Fort Griffin, Dodge City, Ogallala . . . across the lines of states and territories from one end of America to the other.

There would be plenty of opportunity for things to go wrong: rivers to be crossed; storms liable to be endured.

And what was known of the men Dick had hired to

31

look after the all-important herd? The fear came to him, as it had to Faith, that Lyte Grumman might have moved against Dick already through unknown connections, though his pursuit of Faith did argue against it.

In town, Joshua made for the livery barn. In his distracted musings about Faith Hartnett, her mother and the brother who hadn't been in touch, he was negligent of his own safety. It never occurred to him – as it should and normally would have – that Lyte Grumman would have put out word about a stranger riding a big sorrel mare and packing a black-handled Colt Peacemaker.

He failed to note the curious, apprehensive stares of the few folks on the dusty main street or in the old plaza. He thought nothing of the lately hard-ridden, foam-flecked cow ponies with Slash C brands on their hips racked in front of the Black Jack Saloon.

The livery was the usual stables with tall double doors and a loft above. He turned in and was met by a Mexican hostler, a short, pot-bellied fellow with a black moustache and a gold ring in his right ear. He wore cotton overalls, stained and ripped at one knee.

The Mexican took the sorrel's reins from him.

'*Buenas dias, señor*. You stay in town for spell? You want stall for fine cayuse?'

'And groom and grain, *amigo*,' Joshua said.

The hostler held out a stubby-fingered, nail-bitten and grimy hand. It shook nervously and there was a sheen of sweat on his sallow face. 'Two dollar on account, plees.'

32

'That ain't in no wise trusting,' Joshua said.

The Mexican shrugged his rounded shoulders and said gloomily, 'Strange riders, they come, they go – disappear ... Pancho Mestiza must live, you understand, *señor.*'

'I paid tens of dollars for this mare. I don't figure on running out on valuable property and if I did, its sale would pay off any debt.'

Joshua wasn't worried about paying over money to put up his horse, but he was puzzled by Mestiza's jumpy manner. Only at the last moment did he hear footfalls behind him, muffled by the dirty straw and old droppings that littered the barn's runway.

He turned swiftly ... and was faced by three men. They were hard-bitten gunhawk types. Joshua recognized none of them, but guessed instantly that their approach was connected with the gunfight in the graveyard. Their leader's opening words confirmed it.

'The boss wants words an' yuh're comin' with us to the Slash C.'

Joshua's eyes narrowed, judging his chances if guns were pulled. He said truculently, 'I don't reckon so.'

'Mister, yuh'll go where we takes yuh!'

'Nope. You've no legal right to take me anyplace.'

The hardcase sniggered.

'Legal, that's rich! Thar ain't no law aroun' here yuh c'n count on, stranger. Ciudad del Rio is Lyte Grumman's dunghill an' he's top o' the heap. We take yuh – un'erstand?'

Joshua glared back at him angrily, contemptuously. 'Get the hell away from me! I go only where I choose.'

It was then he heard a noise behind him.

He wheeled around just in time to divert the blow of a viciously swung gun butt from his head to his left shoulder. Another Grumman roughneck had already been in the barn, or had come in by a back way.

They must have had the place surrounded. But Joshua wasted no thought on this. He swung a bunched right fist in instant reaction even as numbness flooded down his left arm.

His knuckles smashed into the point of the gun swinger's jaw. The powerful uppercut lifted him off his feet and dumped him in a heap on the mucky floor.

Pancho Mestiza wrung his hands. 'No, *señor*, no! *Por favor* – do as they weesh!'

But Joshua was aroused and merciless.

'You knew they were lying in wait, fatso!'

Without a pause after downing his assailant, he grabbed the hostler and hurled him bodily into the bunch's startled spokesman.

Mestiza and the man he collided with both fell against the sorrel's legs. The horse, still saddled, shied in alarm, whinnied a shrill complaint and danced backwards to a water trough outside the doors in the last of the daylight.

The hovering hands of the two Slash C men who'd been behind the spokesman and were still on their feet said they were thinking about reaching for their irons.

Joshua did some quick calculating. He could take

34

out one of them, maybe both, but the pair on the floor weren't out of the fight and taking on all four would eventually prove a route to disaster.

Additionally, Pancho Mestiza would be more hindrance than help, if not downright hostile.

No way could Joshua get past the entanglements in front of him and through the front doors to his mount. So he sprang for the loft ladder. He scooted up it two rungs at a time.

The gang's leader yelled, 'Hold him! Hold him!'

'I'll kill the bastard!' the punched gun-clubber said, feeling his jaw.

'No! Grumman's orders are to bring him in alive! He don't meet his finish till he's spilled what he's done with the gal!'

A rush was made for the ladder.

'He's trapped hisself anyways.'

'Easy, Butch, the bastard's hell an' lightnin' with a six-gun. . . .'

'Mebbe we should back off, Jed, set fire to this dump . . . smoke him out.'

Pancho Mestiza wailed in horror, his wet-brown eyes wide. 'No, no, *señors* – I have wife and many children. My livery *sustento*—'

'Shuddup, yuh dumb greaser! Butch's jest puttin' a scare in the crazy galoot. He can't get away up thar.'

Jed cautiously mounted the ladder.

In the musty hay heaped in the loft, Joshua had found a pitchfork with rusty but wicked tines. He had an escape plan vaguely formulated, but this was a bonus.

As Jed appeared, he jabbed.

Jed was thrust off the ladder. He hurtled to the hard-packed dirt floor. And he screamed.

'Aw, shit! I've bust m'leg!'

Consternation raged below as Jed's sidekicks clustered round him, arguing about what they should do.

Joshua went directly to the open hayloft doors high above the barn's entrance. Just as he'd recalled, a lifting beam jutted out above them and a rope from the loft ran through a pulley at its far end. Joshua released some more rope from the windlass, before re-securing it.

His left arm was still numb, but he licked his hands and rubbed them together. This was where he took his chances, and nothing in his reckless nature was averse to that.

He shinned down the rope to the pulley, swung himself out wide over the loading platform to the livery runway and dropped. He landed on his feet close to the sorrel mare, who was drinking placidly from the trough.

He vaulted into the saddle from behind, startling the horse into motion.

'Giddup, hoss! We're out of here!'

They pounded down the main street. Butch and the others, except Jed, rushed from the livery, yelling as it hit them he was getting away. Shots were fired, a futile gesture. The mare, despite her day's exertions and recognizing Joshua's urgency, gamely lengthened her pace to a gallop.

As they passed the Black Jack, men in range garb spilled out, alerted by the commotion. Amid shouted exchanges and more useless gunfire, they sprang to the Slash C mounts. In their saddles, they lashed the cow ponies with rein ends and raked them with spurs.

The chase was on.

Joshua thundered out of Ciudad del Rio, the skin crawling on his back. He rode hell for leather into the open country, expecting to feel a bullet any moment.

His only consolation was the knowledge they didn't want to kill him – not outright, not yet. But flying lead couldn't be counted on to show similar discrimination, could it?

His knowledge of the section was dated and at best dim in his memory. The sorrel was weary. The horses of the Slash C crowd, though used some on a fast ride into town, were fresher.

The race for an unknown safety was therefore uneven in more than numbers.

He wheeled the horse off the trail and crashed it through brush, heading for a clump of trees. As a ploy to gain cover, it didn't work. The visible evidence of his passage, if not its sounds, meant his pursuers weren't fooled.

A volley of gunfire raked the brush. Joshua sucked in a sharp breath and ducked instinctively. The mare seemed to falter in her stride. She whinnied and Joshua's heart leaped to his throat, fearing she'd been hit.

The horse recovered and plunged on, but Joshua knew their strategy now: they wouldn't kill him, they'd kill his horse and, being of considerable number, surround and take him prisoner at their subsequent convenience.

He could do nothing about it. He was infuriated by his helplessness. Grumman had been smart enough to figure that any stranger who'd ridden to Ciudad del Rio, and been diverted into a quarrel that didn't really involve him, would ultimately resume his business in the town, whatever that might be. With the day drawing to a close, odds were he'd show up at the livery to stable his horse. In hindsight, this was an obvious conclusion he, Joshua, hadn't been so smart in overlooking.

Maybe he should have kept a weather eye open for trouble. But he hadn't, and it was too late now.

With heart thumping, he rammed his heels into the sorrel's sides, urging her on without any real hope, through the brush and into the trees. The shooting continued. Whining bullets ricocheted through the hardwood timber. He didn't pause to give answering fire, which he knew would be largely ineffective. Inevitably, the hunters closed in and the shot came that did the fatal damage. The sorrel reared with a chilling shriek.

Joshua's feet were out of the stirrups and he slipped from the saddle as the horse collapsed, sinking to earth. He threw himself down behind the body, which kicked once or twice before lying quiet – dead or dying.

His predicament precluded the indulgence of regrets at the loss of a good piece of horseflesh. His enemies had spread out and had him pinned down.

When Joshua tried to move from cover, firing his Peacemaker at no particular target – he had too many opponents and his only aim was at deterrence – responding fire kicked up the sand around his feet. He felt obliged to duck back again. Or be crippled.

He cussed himself long and hard. He hadn't been dogged so much by misfortune as by stupidity. Faith's story had made plain enough Grumman was not a man to cross with impunity. He'd made a mean enemy and failed to appreciate it – as he should have at the outset.

What the hell did he do?

It was a question he was given scant time to ponder. What happened next was out of his hands. Some of the Slash C men must have circled behind the trees, any sound made in their stealthy approach being covered by the pandemonium of continued shooting. Without warning, Joshua was attacked from behind for a second time in less than an hour.

A precisely delivered knock to the head sent him falling to the ground and into what seemed like a deep pit of blackness that swallowed up his senses.

For now, his troubles were over.

4

INTERROGATION

In fleeting interludes of semi-consciousness Joshua was aware of being transported in a jolting wagon. Wrists tied, he was hunched in a painful heap against its tailgate, with blood trickling down his face from somewhere above his left ear and dripping on his pants leg. But most of the time he was lost to a nightmare in which he damned Lyte Grumman in a thick-tongued way that obstructed him from properly articulating the vilest words his disordered brain could produce.

Finally, the raving left him and a sort of sanity returned. His head thumped and he yearned for the blessedness of a peaceful sleep. It wasn't to be. The wagon stopped, the tailgate was dropped, and rough hands supposedly assisted the falling out that left him in a new heap in the dust of an enclosed yard.

Squawking chickens fled. Nearby, dogs set up a furious barking that made his head ring. He smelled cattle and horses. His vision stayed blurred, but though it was the very tail end of the day, there was light enough to ascertain he'd arrived at a hacienda-style ranch headquarters – he presumed the Slash C.

The ranch house itself was big, white-walled, red-roofed. Probably old. It had a gallery across the front behind a series of arches pillared by slender, elegant columns in a grand colonial manner. Above, a second floor had a balcony. No mud-chinked log cabins here. A barn, a bunkhouse, a smithy, a windmill and corrals also looked solidly established, the outbuildings forming a U-shape around the yard.

Entry into the compound was through two massive wooden gates set in a high wall. It was a set-up typical of many ranch houses in the South-west and Mexico.

Flowering pink shrubs grew in wooden tubs along the gallery. A young woman was watering them. She put down the can and hurried over to him and his captors, brushing back strands of black hair blown across her face by the evening breeze.

'What have you done to this man?' she asked the men trying to haul Joshua to his feet.

Maybe not yet in her twenties, she wore corduroy pants and a red silk shirt. Her oval-shaped face had a golden, flawless complexion. She had full, naturally red lips and spoke huskily but in a well-toned voice. Her brown eyes were wide with sympathy and shock. Her heritage, Joshua surmised, was as one with the original Slash C architecture. And at her youthful stage of life it made her a real beauty.

The man supporting Joshua let him slump.

'We done what we was asked, Miss Anna. Your father and Mister Chet's orders. They wanted this man brung in.'

Anna said with a hint of passion, 'My *stepfather's* orders, possibly. Poor Chet is allowed little say. . . .'

She dropped to her knees beside Joshua and cradled his bloodstained head in her arms. She tutted.

'He can't see anyone in this state, Perkins. Carry him into the house – gently – and I'll clean him up. So many brave men to bring in one! You mustn't harm him more – any of you!'

Perkins scowled, his face thunder-cloud black.

'Aw, it weren't more'n a tap on the noggin to make certain-sure he came along quietly. In town, he put Slim's jaw outa joint an' busted Jed's laig. Damn salty! He was askin' fer it.'

Anna sniffed dubiously but prettily. 'Humph! Men!'

Joshua croaked, 'Miss, that'd not be the complete lay of things.' Then, realizing he was God-awful, agonizingly, desperately thirsty, 'I need water, please.'

'You shall have your water,' the girl declared. 'And I'll see if something stronger can be fixed by way of medicine.'

'Obliged, I'm sure,' Joshua mumbled.

Perkins said, 'Mr Grumman mightn't like that—'

The girl snapped back waspishly, 'Must Mr Grumman have the last word on everything that goes on around here? Maybe just for once it wouldn't matter if he didn't!'

Perkins said, 'He is the boss, Miss Anna.'

But he and a partner lugged Joshua into a large kitchen with a stone-flagged floor.

Anna gave him a tin mug of water, bathed the split lump on the side of his head and was about to slash the ties on his wrists with a saw-bladed meat knife when Lyte Grumman showed in person. He glared angrily and his voice was an unpleasant rasp.

'Stop that, Anna! Don't buy into what ain't your affair. Me and the proddy new hardcase in this neck of the woods are going to have us words.'

Joshua said, 'I've got nothing to say you'd want to know. You've no business to hold me here.'

'And I don't want you messing up my house, mister! We'll do this parleying someplace else.'

Grumman turned to Perkins. 'Get some of the boys and take him to the old barn. You know how we get fools that buck us to talk. String him by his tied wrists from the beam!'

Perkins drawled smugly, 'Sure thing, boss.'

Anna caught her breath and her face seemed to pinch and lose its warm glow. But she thought better of framing a further retort.

The girl's opposition didn't escape Grumman's notice. He laughed at her sarcastically.

'You're soft, Anna. Sure as hell you ain't never gonna be a real Grumman. Keep outa the rest of this, hear me? It's the same as playing up to Chet – crowding your luck.'

She nodded, letting her eyes fall from the ugly, pocked and blotched face of her domineering

43

stepfather to the basin of pink-tinted wash water beside her.

'Yes,' she said, 'I-I don't want to know anyhow.'

But the capitulation sounded like sullen obedience, laced perhaps by a dash of fear, not agreement.

Joshua recognized the stripe of his tormentors. Here was a breed of Texas killers that was the best money could buy – leaden-eyed, cruel-lipped, merciless.

'They're experts at loosening tongues and a whole lot else,' Grumman promised him threateningly. 'No one lifts his hand against me and gets away with it. You've been plain lucky till now, and so's that bitch whose game you're playing.'

It was oppressively hot and gloomy in the disused barn and smelled of horses and old manure and burning lamp oil.

Sweating, Joshua saw no glory in denying Grumman the absolute kit and caboodle of what he wanted to know. After taking some painful but not crippling beating, he convincingly allowed that he'd spoken with the girl they'd tried to abduct from the graveyard over in Ciudad del Rio.

He told them a little of what she'd told him – a scrap of information they had to know – but not where he'd taken her. He said he'd heard how Grumman's hired murderers had drygulched Faith Hartnett's father to take control of his graze.

Then, after taking the punishment and feigning grudged admissions, there came surprises.

'Faith *Hartnett*. . . ?' Grumman jeered, the spittle drooling out of a corner of his thick-lipped mouth as he approved of Joshua's battered condition. 'She sold you a bill of goods, feller!'

Joshua licked blood off his own punched and puffy lips. 'What do you mean?' he muttered.

'The bitch's name is *Bloom* – Faith Bloom. Her ma was Belle Bloom who in her heyday was the madam of Ciudad del Rio's bordello. Last time I saw the old cow, she was no more'n a fat, broken-down whore, lavishing the last of her money on grooming her bastard daughter so's she can trap all the boys into making fools of theirselfs.'

Joshua spoke the truth. 'I don't believe you, Grumman. The girl was an innocent, I swear.'

The range hog mocked him with a mirthless, grating laugh.

'Innocent of letting any man have his way maybe. Stand-offish. But full of savvy and trickery. She led on my son, Chet, a spell, and he was fooled likewise. Mister, you'll get nothing but grief outa Faith Bloom. She was in on cheating me outa one thousand head of longhorns, and I mean to get them or the money back.'

Joshua was mystified, but he didn't aim to let it show that he didn't want to believe Grumman's accusations. He had no immediate intention of betraying the young woman he'd saved from a bunch of bullies. His brain was still clouded and he trusted no one.

Grumman's story could contain a degree of truth

45

but it was just as apt to be a clever windy designed to trick him into revealing Faith's whereabouts and plans.

He frowned and let his eyes close. 'Longhorns? Don't understand any of this anyhow. . . .'

'Then you're dumber than I thought, stranger, though you shoot fast and straight, that I'll grant. The young woman you think you was protecting is a liar. Plumb loco in point of fact!'

Grumman jabbed at Joshua's chest for emphasis and spat the lesson into his face, close up.

'See, Faith Bloom despises all men, maybe on account that she lived in a brothel as a button. Can't stand so much as to be touched by a man to tell the truth.'

He turned to his son who was standing by with a sickly grin on his visage and laughed dirtily. 'Ain't that right, Chet? Tell this lunkhead to quit fooling hisself, whatever dreams she's fed him!'

'Yeah, Dad, she's high and mighty all right – but hell, some day she'll have to come down offa her high horse, and am I gonna show her the way of things!'

The lustful gleam in Chet's shifty, deep-set eyes made Joshua more than ever determined to reveal nothing more about Faith, her mother, the house in the hollow, or the missing herd of longhorns.

'I need to check this stuff out,' he said.

Grumman growled. 'You'll check out damn all, mister. You tell us where you've cached the bitch and me and Chet'll do all the checking called for, won't we, boy?'

'Sure, Dad, sure . . . just like you say. I'll make Faith see reason and she'll put us on to her cardsharp pal. All this no-hoper has to do is spill what he done with her and we can take it from there.'

Joshua said with all the force he could summon, 'No deal, kid! Hell can freeze over before I say another word.'

'I figure you still need to learn what end's up,' Grumman snarled, his face darkening. 'Well, that's your last chance for today. You're gonna suffer! And you'll stay here long as it takes, and keep on suffering, till you change your mind, you stubborn sonofabitch.'

His patience used up, he beckoned to his thugs.

'Don't allow him the out of a killing,' he ordered, 'but give him a stronger taste of what he's asking for. When you're done, throw him in the cellar! A day or two of the same and I expect to hear him squealing.'

With a final savage scowl, he turned sharply and stomped out of the barn, followed by Chet.

The sadistic Slash C hardcases carried on with Joshua's punishment where they'd left off, working him over with heavy punches to his body. Strung up as he was, he was helpless to defend himself. He was soon good as dead on his feet, except he wasn't on his feet, which swung several inches above the barn floor as he was jolted by the impacts of the vicious pummelling.

It was a long time since he'd been so brutalized, so hammered. They did it quietly and in no big hurry,

47

placing their chops and blows exactly where they would be most painfully felt, though they cursed once or twice when they hurt their hands.

They kept up the treatment till a supper gong sounded from outside. Then they smashed him into senseless oblivion with a couple of blows that were even more precise, and cut him down.

One of his batterers shook his head in bafflement.

'God-damned idjut! He shoulda let alone what's between Lyte Grumman and the Bloom bitch.'

Although he'd been beaten to a near pulp, at no time had Joshua Dillard cried out or screamed. Other men might have done, but the man who was too tough for the Pinkertons had given no one that satisfaction.

5

FAITH'S NEW DEAL

Faith waited in vain for the arranged return of the man called Joshua Dillard to her mother's forbidding house, hidden away in the tree shadows of the hollow.

After two days, it seemed like it had been too good to be true. The man was just the help the circumstances she'd found herself in demanded. Gun help. He'd drawn his big Colt Peacemaker with blurred speed, leaving the Slash C shootists flatfooted. And recruiting him had required no great effort, thanks to the rough tactics he'd seen employed by the Grummans at the graveyard. In the West – no more nor less than anywhere else whatever conflicting reports – mistreatment of a woman was just what it took to enlist the sympathy of an honourable, square-shooting champion.

But it appeared Joshua Dillard must have ridden on, quitting the whole thing. He'd be far from the first man Lyte Grumman had scared out, or run out, of Ciudad del Rio. It had become that kind of one-man town, while in the country the settlement served one rancher after another had been forced to the wall.

No one had the sand to stand up on their hind legs and fight.

Faith's desperation grew. She had to get to Montana; she had to find Dick, who hadn't been afraid to cock a figurative snoot at the tyrant, besting him in the Black Jack card-room.

'Ma, I fear something must have befallen the Dillard man,' she told her several-chinned mother. 'There's nothing for it – I'll have to go to town again and enquire.'

Belle huffed and puffed; she frowned.

'Have a care, child. You know what happened last time. You were lucky to get away with a whole skin.' She cleared her throat noisily and cackled. 'And ain't it God's truth – you just hate being pawed by menfolks!'

She might be her mother, but Faith resented the gross old woman's cynical amusement.

'It shouldn't be necessary for a female to be so degraded.'

'Would be a whole heap easier and better if you weren't so all-fired set on staying pure!' the mother complained. 'It's nigh on ingratitude and an insult. Maybe you got your nose too high in the air, child. There're more ways to skin a cat, they do say. In Lyte Grumman's case, that crazy, petticoat-chasing son of his would've been a pushover for a girl prepared to pull the tricks.'

Faith shuddered. 'Tricks! Chet! Must you mention that worm?'

Belle rocked her chair some before answering evenly, 'It won't do to forget Chet, Faith. Mark my words and think on it. He must get awful tired of toeing his pa's line.'

Faith didn't let herself be drawn into the argument. The priority was that she had to go after Dick to Montana, and she figured it was out of the question unless she had the services of a man who was prepared to use a gun.

She pulled on a black hooded cloak that achieved the impossible, making her look shapeless and nondescript.

'I'm going into town, Ma. I have to find out what's become of Mr Dillard.'

Nervously, Faith chose the hotel for her first port of call. The front lobby was empty and the register was open on the desk. Taking her luck as she found it, she turned the big, ink-splotched ledger round and flipped back through the last few pages with trembling fingers.

No 'Joshua Dillard', and why would he have used any other name or given her and her mother a false one?

She left the hotel quickly before she could be caught at her prying. Where next?

Of course, the livery barn.

Pancho Mestiza mournfully told what he knew for

a fact about the fighting stranger and what rumour had added.

'*Señorita*, I fear we will not see this *hombre* any more. Señor Grumman's crew, they wait for him. He make big ruckus, break the leg of a *pistolero*. He hightail, but it is said he was brought down by Señor Grumman's crew. Those gunnies *muy enojado*. He prob'ly dead, no?'

It was the worst possible news. Faith felt pale and faint at realization the chance to recoup her losses was lost. In fact, everything was lost.

She was almost without money and Grumman wouldn't let her or her mother work in Ciudad del Rio again. He would eventually locate her and she'd be forced to tell him what she knew of Dick's sly schemes. He and his gun-hands would go after Dick, kill him and claim back the price of a thousand longhorns, a half share of which was indubitably hers. Failure to have collected a profit would then be crystallized. And her purpose served, Lyte Grumman would throw her as punishment to his wolves, to do with as they willed!

Her anxiety progressed into horror, thinking on this fate. She shivered, although the temperature must have been above its ninety-five-degree summer average.

'Are you unwell, *señorita*?' the hostler asked, noting her pallor.

She scarcely heard him and gave only an absent nod. For her mother's advice came back, riding the wave of deep despair, and was tossed on to her strand of black thought.

Don't forget Chet Grumman.

Faith had long lived on her wits. Thinking on her feet – fast – was a talent in which she was well versed.

In times not long past, Chet had pressed his suit with insufferable persistence. She knew he was still intoxicated with her beauty, just as she knew that in his shallowness he really wanted her for just one thing.

But with the far better option of Joshua Dillard no longer around, she might just as easily use him, Chet, for her ends. Handled aright, tempted by the right promises, he could, she reckoned, be bamboozled into helping her find Dick for what would be his own purposes and not his father's.

The daring of her plan was as frightening as its ramifications were potentially distasteful. But what else was left?

She turned to the Mexican hostler.

'Señor Mestiza, have you a pencil and some paper? I have to write a short but very important letter.'

'But of course, *señorita*, anything I have for a beautiful lady. Please come into my office.'

The office was a desk in the corner of a tack room hung with harness, bits of bridles, stirrups and old saddles. The pencil was a chewed stump and the paper was a fly-leaf torn from the back of an out-of-date, San Antonio horse-trader's catalogue.

Faith willed herself to write firmly and carefully in a flowing, copperplate hand, knowing it was the most important invitation she'd made in her life.

When it was written, she folded it tightly and handed it to Mestiza.

'I want to leave this note with you, *señor*. I need it to be delivered when next you see Mr Chet Grumman. You must keep it till you can give it him personally, not to one of his father's hands or even his father himself. It's very – er – private and confidential. . . .'

Mestiza was a romantic, as were many of his race. He sighed.

'*Sí*, I understand perfectly, *señorita!* An affair of the heart. Your secret will rest with me and all will be done as you ask. *No te preocupes!*'

Two evenings later, Faith and Belle heard a rider and his horse coming through the fetlock-deep brush under the drooping and unhealthy trees that surrounded their dump of a house.

Heart thumping, Faith cautiously raised a kitchen blind a smidgeon and looked out through the gap.

It was Chet Grumman sure enough.

He'd successfully followed the directions given in Faith's invitation. She hoped she'd read his nature true; written the right words to ensure his coming was unaccompanied. It looked as though it was. Anyhow, that risk was already taken and too late to reverse.

'Go careful, child! You savvy the sort he is,' her mother said.

She hurried to greet Chet at the door.

'Chet!' she cried, as he swung down from the

saddle. 'I'm so glad you were able to come. I hear I caused your family some bother.'

'You did that,' Chet said warily.

He was transparent as always. Yes, she did have his measure. He hadn't been able to resist her attraction, but he suspected strings were attached to her offer to see him again, tête-à-tête.

'Well, I had to tell you that nothing I've done was directed at you personally, Chet. I've been worrying about that and wouldn't want anything to come between us.'

Chet said in an accusing tone, 'I kinda thought there was everything and nothing between us, Faith. Isn't that what you told me last?'

Faith put her hands to her cheeks as though in confusion.

'Oh, I've been so silly! Do come in and let me explain.'

They entered the house and the front parlour.

Chet nodded to Belle, taking off his hat. 'Howdy, ma'am.'

The fat old woman acknowledged him. 'Ah, young Mr Grumman. Always a pleasure to entertain a gentleman, isn't it, Faith?'

'Oh, yes, Mama,' Faith said primly.

She took off her wrap to reveal the flattering dress she'd been wearing for all of two days in hopeful anticipation of Chet's visit. The gown was of the finest, lightest pink silk and was fit for a ball. It had been made to measure by an expert seamstress to a very fashionable pattern. A high waist and deeply cut bodice tightly sheathed and accentuated her fullness while allowing a tantalizing view of bare skin.

Chet was unable to suppress a gasp. It was like seeing a rose growing in a cesspit.

Before his speechlessness could extend into embarrassment, Faith said, 'My attitude is that you should always have the best you can afford. It's something I guess your father doesn't allow you to practise.'

'What's my pa gotta do with this?' Chet said defensively.

Belle wheezed in what was evidently intended as polite mirth and put in her two cents' worth.

'A hard man, your pa, Mr Grumman, but you'll know that, I'm sure. Keeps you on a tight rein, don't he? Orders you about like a kid.'

Not wanting to offend the dazzling vision that was Faith by insulting her busybody mother, whom he knew was nothing but the retired manager of a whorehouse, he said, 'Suppose he does.'

Faith took it as a question.

'Of course he does!' she said brightly. 'We're all in that boat – everyone around afraid to lift a finger against the all-powerful Lyte Grumman, except Dick.'

'Dick cheated at cards,' Chet said flatly. 'Robbed him. And you helped in it.'

'Sure, Dick took what was owed *all* of us, Chet. But he's run off with his winnings. I'd claim them back, except it means following him to Montana where he has gone. That's no job for a girl on her own. But if she was sided by a strong man – a man who was his own man – perhaps it would be different. . . .'

She let the suggestion hover.

Chet was besotted with her beauty, driven wild by her untouchability, but he wasn't stupid. He frowned in puzzlement.

'You proposing I go with you to get back that loot? You saying Dick's dumped you and it's my pa that keeps us apart?'

Faith said, as though considering, 'Those are interesting ideas, Chet.' Then she threw up her hands sadly in dismissal. 'No, it can never be! You have Anna Carranza, don't you? Perhaps your father intends you should one day be wedded to her. It wouldn't do for you to be seen as having some other woman, and it would make Anna jealous.'

As Faith hoped, Chet saw the unexpected but alluring promise of somehow possessing Faith. He suddenly whipped around and headed for the horizon.

Heatedly, he said, 'I'm sick of my Mex stepsister! She can't hold a candle to a pure white beauty like you. She throws herself at my head. It ain't Pa's plan she should, but her own. Pa's her legal guardian till she's of age, or married. She figures to get away from him through me – that's all there is to that.'

'Oh, I'm sure there's more,' Faith demurred. 'I think Anna's truly infatuated with you. And one day you'll inherit your father's wealth and power, not to mention the lands that came to him when he married Anna's widowed mother.'

Chet tore at his hair. 'Aw, hell . . . wish I was free of the whole goddamned mess!'

'But you can be,' Faith said gently. 'The alternative is plain. We'll find Dick together, do away with him and we'll have all that herd money for ourselves, to build other lives.'

Belle's chair creaked as she rocked it with approving vigour and a fat and meaningful smile.

'Oh, listen to her! My daughter is a smart girl, Mr Chet Grumman!'

Chet was on the edge of accepting the proposal, but the last doubts still crowded him.

'We do this and how do I know you won't run out on me when we've gotten the dinero? Leave me at my Pa's mercy – betray me to the law maybe. . . . Nope, I can't do it.'

'Oh, Chet!' Faith said, with all the passion she could simulate. 'You still don't understand, do you? I want it to be a new start for us . . . free of the Lyte Grummans and the Dicks and the Annas.'

'Yeah, sure. We're both in a tight spot of a different sort, but how do I know you're playing square?'

She played her last card. 'If you agree to take me to Montana, I'll agree to be your wife.'

He chewed his lower lip.

His greedy thinking was visible to her on his face: Dick dead, and the money, his freedom, plus the stunning girl he'd always wanted, would be his . . . legally tied to him for all time, unable to testify against him.

'All right, it's a deal,' he said. 'I ain't so fooled as to believe your offer's in answer to my fatal fascination, but it makes a kind of sense and there could be plenty in it for both of us. Why, I ain't no Fancy Dan gambler like Dick, but I'll enjoy making you a red-blooded *man's* woman!'

Faith suppressed a shiver, vowing to herself she'd find a way never to let the consummation come to pass.

'That's an honest thought, Chet,' she managed to get out.

Over the next half-hour, they sat together at a rough pine table and refined arrangements, which were largely those Faith had made with Joshua Dillard, though with daunting modifications it was going to need all her courage to face.

When Chet Grumman had left, Belle lurched out of her rocking chair and poured herself a celebratory drink, cackling and wheezing happily over her girl's machinations and the recruitment of a substitute sucker.

'The fast gun failed, but I still have Faith!'

6

JEALOUS ANNA

Down in the cellar at the Slash C, Joshua Dillard had no way of measuring time. They brought him jerky, hard tack and water – trail-rations food – though once there was a tepid, watery concoction that was a poor imitation of sonofabitch stew made from organ meats. The scraps they gave the ranch dogs were probably better.

Were these poor meals regular? He guessed not. So he figured anything between four and six days might have passed.

Repeatedly, he was asked whether he was ready to talk to the boss, meaning Lyte Grumman.

Talk? And then what happens, he asked himself, fingering his puffed and smashed lips. Purpose served, would the brains Grumman had tried to pick be blown out; did he quietly disappear, buried maybe in some unmarked grave on the vast Slash C range?

Every time he said no, which sometimes earned

him a further slapping-about and a kicking, but in
the cramped confines of the cellar it was nothing like
the beating in the barn. Grumman conceivably
imagined time was on his side; that eventually, tired
of incarceration, he would crack and tell what he
knew about the girl who'd claimed to be Faith
Hartnett with a brother called Dick.

A continuous discomfort of his captivity was the
airlessness. The small cellar wasn't deep enough to
provide relief from the summer heat. Rather, with
constant human habitation for which it hadn't been
designed, it seemed to do the opposite, intensifying
a sweaty, earthy humidity with little circulation of air
to dry it out.

A compensation was that the various wounds he'd
sustained were healing naturally with enforced rest
and the passing of time. No longer did he wake up to
the hellish pain of terrible bruises, cuts, splits and
abrasions.

He gave thought to escape, but it produced no
workable ideas. Therefore, he was compelled to play
the patient waiting game till, he hoped, some
changed circumstance or slip-up on the part of his
jailers gave him his chance.

It was the story of his life, Joshua concluded: 'You
lose again.' He chose all the wrong cases and causes.
Mostly, the few bucks he earned were eaten up by his
expenses and the task of keeping himself alive on
Western frontiers with no regular basis of support.
The intervals when he had money to spare in his
pockets were few. The Bennett affair in Colorado

had provided one of them but that was now quickly becoming history.

Maybe he'd been born under an evil star.

His dark musings were broken by the rasp and click of withdrawn bolts and squeak of the hinges of the opening trapdoor. A draught of fresher air and a narrow shaft of lamplight from the room above entered his prison.

'Mister Dillard?' a voice said enquiringly, softly.

He recognized the voice as belonging to the young woman who'd showed him kindness by tending his hurts on his arrival at Grumman's headquarters. They'd called her Anna; she'd acknowledged Lyte Grumman was her stepfather, and the man had dismissed her peremptorily. Ordered her to keep out. . . .

So what was she doing here? Joshua's hopes were kindled at last.

'Yes, that's my name,' he said quietly. 'And they call you Anna. What do you want?'

'Please, I-I'm coming down. I want to talk.'

'Seems everybody wants talk. I've nothing much to say, but you're welcome.'

It struck him as intriguingly topsy-turvy – granting one of his captor's relatives permission to enter his prison and speak to him.

The slim, dark Hispanic girl opened the trap wider and slipped in lithely. She struck a vesta and held its leaping flame to a candle. She lowered the trap gently and came down the ladder leaning against the earthen wall.

'Poor man,' she said. 'They have treated you very badly, whatever you did. Here, you must drink and eat something decent.'

In a gunnysack, she'd brought a flask of brandy, a canteen of chilled milk and freshly baked biscuits that were way better than anything he'd yet been served on the Slash C.

'Much obliged, miss, but what is this? Your stepfather said you weren't to interfere.'

'Lyte Grumman is a pig!' she said emphatically. 'I know he has you prisoner because of the herd that was stolen off him in the famous poker game at the Black Jack. I was glad about that!'

Joshua was as baffled as ever. He shook his head.

'How do you fit into all this, young lady?'

'I am Anna Carranza and my father was Juan Carranza, whose family once owned the lands that became known as the Slash C. After the annexation of Texas, my people were viewed as a conquered people, like the Indians. But my mother was very beautiful. When my true father died, she remarried Lyte Grumman who was also a widower. It was a terrible mistake. All that really interested Grumman was the ranch the marriage brought him. I think my mother died of a broken heart.'

Joshua frowned. His own brief encounters with Lyte Grumman had shown him a man consumed by avarice and ruthless self-interest. As much had been written on the cattleman's ugly face.

'A sad history, but it is history. How can helping me help you?'

The girl's expression turned petulant, marring her prettiness. Leastwise, that was how it looked to Joshua in the flicker of the candlelight.

'Mister Grumman is my legal guardian and an autocratic bully who wants to rule my life! He has a wonderful son, Chet, who is quite unlike him and like me is his virtual slave!'

Joshua hadn't, as he recalled, been struck by any sterling qualities in the junior Grumman, but Anna was young and the young could be foolish in their romantic imaginings about members of the opposite sex, especially when deprived of a range of suitable company. All Anna Carranza probably had in common with Chet was a dislike of tyrannical old Lyte's hold over their lives.

He made no comment beyond the barest nod and let her blaze on.

'One day I wish to marry Chet, but I know his father forbids it. He does not want anyone with Carranza blood to regain any portion of the property that Chet must some day inherit.'

Joshua coughed at the folly of the girl's marital ambitions and took a gulp of the brandy to harden his heart for the task of convincing her she was misguided.

'Are you sure about all this? What does Chet say?'

'Chet can say nothing!' She was exasperated by the questions, as he'd thought she would be.

'Chet is a man, of course,' she added, in a tone of assumed wisdom. 'Naturally, he looks for other outlets, which is how Faith Bloom got her hooks into him.'

Remembering Faith's report of Chet's odious pestering, Joshua's eyes widened. He suggested, 'Maybe that was only how it looked to you. . . .'

But Anna was carrying herself away in a frenzy of flashing-eyed, Latin jealousy.

'No! I know it is so. With her fine clothes and her temptress's ways, she has turned his head!'

'You have evidence of this?'

'Of course!' she said triumphantly. 'Chet has vanished, just like Faith Bloom. He must have left me to elope with her . . . to go together after Dick Redvers and claim her share in the money from the herd the pair stole from Chet's father. Then Chet will never come back. He will be lost both to his father and me! I will never become mistress of the Slash C. It is why I must turn to you – the only brave and independent man on this spread!'

'I don't get the half of it . . .' Joshua muttered.

'But you were also told lies by this horrible Bloom woman, were you not? Like her, you know where the trickster Dick Redvers has gone. If I help you escape from here, you can go after them, recover the Slash C herd money and free Chet from the siren's clutches!'

Joshua surveyed the girl yet more curiously.

'Is that so? But Faith told me her name was Hartnett and that the Dick who won your stepfather's cows in a poker session wasn't a Redvers but her brother, Dick Hartnett. And that Dick quit Texas, driving the herd to Montana and hasn't been heard from since. She and her ma were left hiding out, beside themselves with worry and near destitute.'

Anna raised clenched hands in frustration.

'Aagh! You must understand!' she blurted.

'I wish I could.'

After waving both hands helplessly in the air, she let them fall to her sides.

'Very well. I agree that Faith has had no money from the cattle and that she wants to hunt down Dick, but the rest of what she told you is a string of falsehoods, carefully put together to match some of the truth.'

'You might be mistaken.'

'I am not!'

'Then maybe you can give me some proof your version of the story is the correct one. Else, it would be less than fair of me to accept your offer of help on expectations I'd no intention of fulfilling. I can't go chasing across the land for nothing on one girl's say-so. Surely you can appreciate that.'

She gave a deep and pained sigh. But after she'd remained silent for a moment, her face lit up.

'If you won't believe me, perhaps you will Nate Quentin,' she said rapidly.

'Nate Quentin?'

'He's a crippled old cowpuncher who was Tom Hartnett's foreman. I'll help you escape and you can go book into the hotel in Ciudad del Rio under another name. It's night, but the moon is up and I've saddled a horse you may safely take. I also found the big revolver they took off you. You must wait in your hotel room and be constantly on your guard. As soon as I'm able, I'll arrange a meeting with old Nate and take you to meet him at his shack. He'll verify every word of what I've told you – and tell you more, I think.'

Joshua could see potential flaws in Anna's swiftly devised plan of introduction to an independent informant, but in the balance his misgivings about continuing to languish in a cellar outweighed them.

Anna's tenacity and youthful optimism made it hard for him to refuse her appeals. Also, he felt sorry about the oppressive circumstances in which she lived on this place, while her plainly misguided worship of Chet Grumman suggested she was in need of education, and maybe protection.

'All right,' he said gruffly. 'I might as well do it. I want to get to the bottom of this fol-de-rol anyhow.'

Above the cellar, Joshua found himself in a shed housing a wagon. He went straight away to the wagon's toolbox. Fixed to the left side in back of the lazyboard, it pulled out in front of the rear left wheel and contained a hatchet, spare bolts and pins, a small saw, some rope . . . and a screwdriver.

'Ah-hah!'

'What are you doing?' Anna asked.

'You'll see.'

He returned to the trapdoor and worked out half the length of the screws holding the two heavy bolts. He lowered the trap, slid home its bolts, then lifted it as far as the loosened screws would allow, gripped its edge and wrenched upwards mightily.

After a couple of heaves, the bolts ripped loose

from their fixings, leaving splintery evidence to suggest the trap had been forced open by brute force from within.

'You're wasting time,' Anna said. 'I don't see the purpose you've served.'

'Supposing your stepfather is told I must've had help to get out. Suspicion could fall on you. What do you figure he might do?'

Anna tossed her head proudly, making the candle flame catch highlights in her sleek dark hair.

'I don't care!'

'Hmm . . . I do. Thisaway there'll be less call for anyone to figure I had help.'

'I know how to be brave and silent, too!'

Worried by her naïvety, Joshua shook his head.

'Remember, I've had a dose of the suffering he can be minded to hand out. I also saw his men getting rough with Faith. It's how I got into this mess. So I don't reckon he'd go easy on you, either. I'd purely hate to know any woman had paid for my freedom like that.'

Anna swallowed audibly, but didn't answer back.

Joshua said, 'Now, be a good girl and bring around that horse, if you will!'

No man saw him ride away from the Slash C in the white, bright moonlight, hitting the trail for Ciudad del Rio and pushing along at a sharp gait on a suitably chosen, docile cow-pony.

He was glad to feel the familiar weight of his worn-handled Peacemaker at his hip. It was a mighty fine gun and Anna had done well to think of retrieving it from her father's office and restoring it to him. She'd also returned to him most of his confiscated dollars.

He congratulated himself, too, on taking measures to avoid leaving the girl in danger. His code had told him it was the necessary thing, the right thing, to do.

But had it been enough?

Ahead, all manner of shadows grew deeper, blacker.

7

A DIFFERENT FAITH

In the stagnant heat of the hotel room, Joshua Dillard waited.

He waited. He waited. . . .

One day became two and then three. He showed himself only passingly to buy food to take out from the café. Thankfully, he reacquainted himself with roast beef and potatoes, bacon, beans and coffee. He trusted to luck that no one at the café would connect him with the man who'd been involved in the fracas at the livery barn and been chased out of town by the hard-bitten Slash C gun crew. And who'd disappeared. . . .

No one wanted to look into that. No one wanted to know. The people of Ciudad del Rio never interfered in the affairs of Lyte Grumman.

Lying on a lumpy bed, staring up at the ceiling

boards, shadowy and cobwebbed, with the window blinds down, was better most ways than being in a cellar dug in the earth, like an animal trapped in a pit. And the rest was good for him, of course, though after the luxury of washing and shaving, the reflection in a cracked, brown-specked mirror remained of a gaunt face with bloodshot eyes and deep-etched lines of fatigue.

He felt in improved shape, but it did get to a thinking man, worrying about what might be happening out there.

The missing gun did it. Lyte Grumman had kept the complete rig in his office and – though he hired many rogues known for fingers that were as light as they were swift in clearing a gun from leather – he didn't think any of his crew would have had the gall, opportunity or motive to steal the battered but well kept and cleaned Colt Peacemaker taken off Joshua Dillard.

He studied on it. Speculation narrowed his muddy eyes and creased his dirty-skinned face. The range hog remembered how his stepdaughter had taken it upon herself to bathe this Dillard fellow's cut head on the day of his arrival.

A sum of money had also been taken from his well-filled cash box.

A ranch hand's movements within his boss's house would be noticeable. The men's living quarters were the bunkhouse. Contrarily, Anna was at home in the ranch house. In fact, Grumman resented the paradox that she seemed more at home in the place than he, its legal master.

'For God's sake . . .' he muttered to himself.

Grumman summoned three of his trustiest henchmen: Hank Roache, Kurt Schwimmer and Luis Alvarez.

'I don't savvy how Dillard could've smashed his way outa the cellar,' he said. 'There's been mischief-doing here. I reckon the bastard was let out.'

'Ain't none o' the boys'd pull a crazy stunt like that,' Schwimmer said.

'Guess not.'

'Then who the hell. . . ?'

Grumman pursed his lips and his voice thickened with disgust. 'My late second wife's greaser daughter, Anna Carranza.'

'She told yuh?'

'Nope, and I ain't wasting breath asking. We'll watch. More exactly, you three are gonna take turns watching and following, so's she don't figure we're on to her game. If I'm right, mebbe she'll lead us to Dillard. He'll get his proper needings next time.'

Alvarez licked his lips.

'What about Anna?'

'Yeah, Luis, it's time the treacherous little she-cat got her comeuppance. A horsewhipping for the pair of 'em! See if that'll get Dillard to squawk. Mebbe when he has, a bullet to follow. He'll need to be eliminated.'

'And Anna?' Alvarez said, wild-eyed and slobbering in his eagerness.

'Mebbe not killed.'

'But we do what we like, hey?'

'Yeah, yeah. Whatever . . . If she goes to Dillard, it proves she's sold out on the Slash C. Treat her like an *hombre* would a *puta!* A woman who ain't married on a spread like this is apt to be trouble anyways. No offence meant, but it ain't handy when half the goddamn crew's a-bellowing an' pawing up dust.'

A roster was organized for the shadowing of Anna.

As the three hardcases made to leave, Schwimmer turned and broke other news.

'Aw yeah, another thing, boss. One of the crew had to drag a cow outa the mud in Surota Hollow. He reckons he stumbled acrost Belle Bloom, hidin' out down thar in a ruined house. Could be she'll know where her daughter has run off.'

He then came as close to embarrassment as was possible for an outlaw of his stripe.

'Mebbe she'll know where Chet is likewise.'

On the third day holed up in Ciudad del Rio, Joshua had a visitor to his hotel room. Anna Carranza had finally been able to keep her word.

'Nate Quentin despises Lyte Grumman and his thugs as much as I,' she told him. 'He said he'd be pleased to tell you all he knows and you'll see I've told nothing but the truth.'

She'd come in a two-seater red and black Studebaker buggy. The black cow-pony that had brought Joshua had been set loose outside town on the night of his arrival, to trot back to its home corral

73

where Anna had sneaked out at first light to off-saddle it.

Joshua sat beside her on the leather-covered buggy seat and they rolled out of town. To go visiting, she was wearing a feminine dress in place of work shirt and corduroy pants. The girl had an unsettling effect on him, unlike the usual run of pretty girls of his ever-changing acquaintance in a nomadic life.

She was very composed, in a stiff-backed, grave manner. Her face was straight-lipped and solemn. Last time he'd been with her, her dark eyes had flashed with frustration, even anger at his reluctance to believe her tale. Today, they were calm, lustrous pools filled not with wisdom – she was too young to have it – but with the sureness of her coming vindication.

Her black hair fluttered like a pennant behind her in the breeze of the slipstream.

An hour's rapid, wheel-whirring running went by and they came to a place where prairie-like country gave way to stands of pine and juniper brakes. Joshua knew this country only vaguely.

Quentin's shack, half-hidden in a tangle of prickly-leaved and dark-berried brush, had about it a look of desertion ... till careful second scrutiny when sharper eyes detected against a backdrop of greenery and vivid blue sky the almost invisible wisps of white smoke lifting lazily and thinly from the adobe chimney. A cook fire, Joshua guessed, since it was mid-morning of a hot summer day.

A brooding quiet hung over the place, seeming to

press heavily on the ears after the clatter of the horse's hoofs and the crunch of iron-rimmed buggy wheels on the rough side-trail to the shack.

Anna frowned. 'The scrub jays are very quiet.'

She didn't explain the remark but hullooed the silent house.

The latch of the unpainted pine-plank door lifted with a snap. The door scuffed the stamped-dirt floor as it opened on leather hinges. Nate Quentin made his appearance, blinking his eyes against the strong sunlight, a shotgun in his hands.

The eyes were watery; the hands were twisted by rheumatism.

'Hah! It's you, Anna. Come on in, an' bring the gent with yuh.'

'Well, who did you think it might be, Mr Quentin? Why the ten-gauge?'

'Been lurkers in the brakes since you was here yesterday. Fiddlefooted scum, I guess, passin' through, checkin' the place out. Ain't nothin' here for 'em, that's fer sure.'

They went into the shack. It was a one-room, primitive construction of logs chinked with mud, presently filled with the aroma of roasting meat.

A carved wooden plaque was tacked over an unpolished but scrubbed table. Its text read:

Trust in the LORD with all thine heart; and lean not unto thine own understanding.

Close up, Joshua assessed Nate Quentin was not so

much 'old' as in late middle age and broken-down. His legs were bowed and one looked a mite shorter than the other, which caused him to move with a pronounced limp. The washed-out eyes were of indeterminate colour in a lined face and he wore whipcord pants and a checked shirt under a scratched cowhide vest.

'You the feller as wants to hear about my ol' boss, Tom Hartnett?'

'I would surely be obliged, sir. About all the Hartnetts.'

Quentin looked at him perplexed. 'Weren't never but the one as I knew of.'

'How about his daughter, his son?'

He squinted. 'You got the wrong Hartnett, mister. The one buried beside the Ciudad del Rio mission was never married, an' he weren't the sort to have got on the wrong side o' the sheets. A fine man, an upright man, was Tom.'

'Maybe before you knew him?'

Quentin shook his head vigorously. 'I were ramrod of the Circle H fer years, mister.'

'Strange. Anna may have mentioned I met a young woman called Faith and her mother Belle. I understood they were Hartnetts – that they had a brother and son, Dick.'

'Yuh run too darned silty fer me to see what yuh're drivin' at. . . . Pour the cawfee, Anna.'

The girl dutifully took down three tin cups from a shelf and lifted a steaming granite pot from the back of the stove.

76

'The *Hartnetts*,' Joshua insisted.

Quentin repeated the names, musing on them.

'Belle . . . Faith . . . Dick. Yeah, those names mean something put together in this neck o' the woods.' He heaved a sigh and tutted critically.

Joshua remembered what Lyte Grumman had told him. He'd found the story then difficult to accept, suspecting its extravagances were inspired by the range-hog's prejudice and animosity. Now he figured he was going to hear something similar from an independent source.

'Do tell,' he said. A sinking feeling in his stomach told him he was about to learn Faith had indeed fooled him. 'Tell me the whole story. Take your time.'

The crippled cowman stared into the shimmer of heat over the stove, but he was looking someplace else, maybe into the past.

'Belle Bloom ran a whorehouse in Ciudad del Rio. Your local girls' boarding-house, caterin' fer the local clientele an' the riders driftin' through. A smart, shrewd madam with a bit o' glamour thrown in. Hard, but a looker in her day like she ain't anymore.'

He acknowledged the mug of coffee Anna pressed upon him with the sparest nod.

'She had no regular man, but she had a gal-child, a button she called Faith. The gal was raised a proper lady. Far as I know, she had nothin' to do with the whorin'. Fact, on account o' what she must've sometimes seen, she kinda despised an' shunned men on that level. She weren't gonna grow up no loose, bawdy-house woman.'

77

Anna urged, 'Tell Mr Dillard what she did do.'

'After her ma got old an' fat an' sick, she took work in the Black Jack card-room as dealer, hostess or somesuch. Gamblin', in a room that had gents in number with minds occupied else'n by ladies o' the night, was a vice she must've opined was all right, yuh unnerstand?'

Joshua lifted a sardonic eyebrow.

'The inequality of the dens of iniquity, I guess.'

Quentin didn't hear or didn't appreciate his remark.

He shrugged, sipped his coffee absently and went on, 'At the Black Jack, a tinhorn card-sharp called Dick Redvers came into the picture. Youngish, a Fancy Dan feller with soft hands that never knew real work.'

He paused to flex and examine his own left hand, contrarily gnarled and calloused.

Joshua had known many professional Western gamblers in his time and had once posed as a faro dealer in the course of a memorable case. It wasn't hard to get a fix on the type in his mind: an indoors man in an outdoors world. Doubtless he could shoot and ride if occasion demanded, but he wouldn't know how to rope a cow or hunt for game.

'This Redvers lived by his wits an' was eaten up by the makin' o' money. He took enough offa the suckers, but he didn't spend much 'cept on the clothes an' trimmin's that allowed him to keep up the appearances o' his trade. Anyhow – an' I'm guessin' a bit here – Faith Bloom teamed up with him, likely reckonin' on securin' a cut o' his takin's to spend on her own finery. They were a matched pair thataway.

'Dick Redvers prob'ly wanted to bed her – many did – but she'd've stood fer none o' that. Day came when Redvers and Faith Bloom pulled their big coup. Dick walked from the table with a mighty rich pot that held a big part o' the Slash C herd.'

'The cattle he has now driven or is driving to Montana,' Joshua put in.

Quentin scoffed. 'Any 'puncher in this neck o' the woods would know that fer a lie, mister. Redvers hired some grub-line riders an' took the cows to the railhead stockyard in San Antonio. He sold the critters to a cattle buyer fer a good price an' they was shipped out on the Galveston, Harrisburg and San Antonio Railway. I swear to Almighty God that's the truth. Yuh c'n check it out if'n yuh don't believe me.'

Joshua admitted he did believe him, hard though it was since it also meant admitting to himself he'd been taken in completely by Faith's lies.

'So what happened after that?' he asked.

'Redvers, lit out, vamoosed, hightailed it. My figurin'd be he'd gotten tired o' havin' his amorous inclinations cold-shouldered by Faith. With all that money from their joint efforts stuffin' his bags, he ditched his pardner an' went on alone. Mebbe like yuh said, he's gone up to Montanny. It's fur enough away.'

From outside, the peace in the shack was interrupted by raucous, slightly metallic and sharply inflected bird-cries. The jays had broken the eerie silence that overhung the place.

Joshua tensed, realizing he should have given attention earlier to the strangeness of that.

The crestless blue-and-grey scrub jays native to the region were characteristically social birds, vocal and conspicuous, jerking their bodies up and down on every call note.

But these alarmed cries he was hearing now became a rapid series of harsh and scratchy, staccato notes. Someone was invading their territory, possibly disturbing their nests which were sometimes no more than four feet off the ground.

Nate Quentin lurched for his shotgun.

'They're a-comin' through the scrub! The scum's a-comin!'

8

'HOW SUDDEN DO YOU WANT TO DIE?'

Anna rushed to the window. Joshua, at her elbow, pulled her to one side, so she was behind the cover of the primitive burlap curtains.

'Careful!' he said.

Anna gasped and let the quick breath out again in a rush.

'Slash C gunnies – the worst, Hank Roache, Kurt Schwimmer and I think Luis Alvarez. They must have followed us!'

Joshua shook his head, confident that wasn't the case.

'No one followed today. They must've done it last time you came.'

'Oh! How could they have known?'

He figured out the how quickly.

'Maybe they guessed you were the one who set me

81

loose. Tracked you, lay in wait for me.'

Anna trembled. 'For us! Grumman would have sent them, surely. If I'm found with you, they'll punish me, too!'

Meanwhile, before Joshua or Anna could stop him, Nat Quentin flung open his door and strode out to confront the newcomers, putting his trust not in the Lord but in his ten-gauge.

It was poor judgement, the very worst of judgement.

'Hold it thar, yuh varmints!' he hollered. 'Git away from my house, an' git quick, or I'll pepper your hide with two barrels o' birdshot!'

He cocked the right hammer.

'Put down that scattergun, yuh old fool!' Schwimmer yelled back.

But Luis Alvarez had no patience with the nicety of warnings. By his reckoning, a man who cocked a gun and aimed it in his direction wasn't given chances; shown any mercy. If the opposing gunman had three enemies to watch, so much the easier for him.

He drew his six-gun fast and smooth, cocking and firing in one fluid motion.

The shotgun boomed a split-second later but Quentin was already stumbling, mortally hit, and the pellets sprayed only the brush, shredding a useless swathe across the foliage.

Anna screamed.

Jays flung up into the sky with a rapid flapping.

'We're caught dead to rights!' Joshua said.

'What do we do? They've killed Nate Quentin.

Shot a harmless, stove-up old cowpuncher in cold blood. Now they have to kill us!'

In her horror she had overlooked that Quentin had menaced them with a double-barrelled shotgun.

The jays settled into wheeling glides on fifteen-inch wingspans. Noisy cries rasped from their throats.

Joshua, thinking fast, could come up with only one desperate suggestion. Ciudad del Rio was a little town, but not all the people in it could be so damn little as to be under Grumman's thumb.

'I'll try to delay them, hold them off. You go out the back window and try to circle round through the brush to the buggy. Once you make it . . . head for Ciudad del Rio lickety-spit! Grumman can't have the whole town treed. Go to people you know in the 'dobe quarter.'

'What about you?'

'Don't worry about me. Let me look after myself.'

'I can't do that!'

'Then you're a loco fool! You stay, we both die. Only question's how sudden. Go to it, you dumb idiot, go!'

His rough, disparaging words as much as his terseness persuaded her. It was, as Joshua had calculated, very wounding to the Hispanic girl's feelings to be spoken to so brusquely.

Somehow, the insult counteracted the paralysis of her fear. She gathered her wits and leaped into lithe motion, using a chair to assist her unorthodox exit. She raised her skirts and, slim legs flashing, scrambled over the sawn-lumber sill to drop lightly to the soft earth outside.

Left alone with his thoughts and the danger, Joshua's silent prayer was that for Anna's sake the three now out front were the only Grumman hardcases in the offing.

Schwimmer called to them.

'Dillard! Anna! We know yuh're in thar! Come on out, hands high!'

Joshua bawled back, hoping to smother any sound Anna might make pushing through the brush.

'You had no call to kill Nate Quentin. We're staying put, you murdering bastards! You want us, come on in!'

Roache said, 'We jest might, Dillard.'

Unconsciously, Schwimmer repeated Joshua's own words. 'Ain't no skin offa our noses how sudden yuh die!'

Peering round the window frame, Joshua saw spittle drool from Luis Alvarez's lips as he laughed excitely to his sidekicks.

'Have a care, *hombres*! Remember, we will show the uppity Miss Carranza her place before we send her to hell!'

But Schwimmer, glimpsing the edge of Joshua's profile at the window, drew his lips back from his teeth in a snarl. His gun was in his hand and he used it.

The bullet would have spattered Joshua's brains all around the shack if it had hit him.

But it missed by a hair's-breadth. Joshua had

jerked back.

The bullet whistled past him and slammed through the plaque carved with the *Trust in the LORD* text and into the log wall. The plaque – Nate Quentin's failed talisman, kind of – cracked in two and fell. Lumber behind splintered.

Joshua lifted his Peacemaker and snapped a reply, blindly, unaimed, through the window opening. He had no hope for the shot other than it would create further diversion and din.

The trio had advanced past Anna's buggy and were between it and Quentin's shack. If he could keep all their attention and they didn't look back, he might win Anna her chance.

The need for action was pressing. Yet Joshua was powerless. To risk shooting his way out of Quentin's shack would serve no purpose.

It was absolutely necessary to draw them in; to keep them distracted as long as he stayed on his feet, unhit by their return gunfire.

Hell, wasn't it always the same? He hadn't owed any of these people anything, but he'd ended up putting his life on the line with no prospect of putting money in his pocket at the end.

It was the story of his life, getting dragged into this or that peck of troubles and having to fight his way out. Often as not, he'd be stony broke come the reckoning.

This time, he'd stepped in first off, as any decent gent would, to save a young woman being harassed by male bullies in a graveyard where he'd been going

about his own innocent business. But Faith Bloom
had led him down the road a long piece. It was
incredible that anyone could lie so well, yet that was
what she'd done. Little doubt about it now, he
reflected sourly.

Maybe listening to her at all hadn't been so smart.
He'd had her pegged for an injured party. She wasn't
and she was, and she could finish up a whole lot
worse, wherever she was.

Meanwhile, another young woman, Anna
Carranza, had seemingly saved his bacon and told
him a story quite different from Faith's, only to pitch
him into a further predicament – a mess of even
more desperate trouble. The grimness of this
situation was evidenced by the inert body of the
former Hartnett ramrod, lying shot dead on his
shack's threshold.

The echoes of Joshua's wild shot died.

Hank Roache called, 'Yuh're stickin' your neck
way out, Dillard! Yuh think yuh're hard, but Ol' Man
Grumman is harder – the hardest *hombre* you ever
saw. Buckin' him ain't good at all, no sir! Better come
along real easy. That sassy gal, likewise. She's gonna
get her ass whipped!'

Alvarez said, 'And that will not be all!'

'Don't make a lick o' sense coverin' her backside,
Dillard. Those is the orders. She's gotten you an'
herself inta a hole she can't get out of.'

Alvarez laughed evilly. 'But we will get into hers for
sure, *hombre*!'

Blather on, you slavering fools, Joshua implored

86

silently. He'd seen Anna at the fringe of the circling brush to the far left. One more moment, a few steps closer to the shack by the threat-making hardcases, and she would have the chance to make her dash.

'That's no square shake, greaser!' he said, talking for time. 'We want better terms before we quit this fight.'

Schwimmer said in scornful disbelief, 'Yuh're in no place t' dictate none, mister!'

Anna disappeared again and Joshua's uneasiness increased. How much more could he clear her way?

'I'm dead against letting you men molest any woman. Grumman's orders be damned! They're plumb disgusting!'

As he finished shouting defiance, Anna made her play. She sprinted from the brush to the buggy, scratched brown legs and arms pumping, leaped to its seat, threw off the brake and pulled the whip from the bracket.

With a near-breathless cry, she lashed the horse wildly into a trot – then a canter – a gallop. . . .

The Grumman toughs turned, caught by surprise and unsure how they should deal with the development.

'Hey! The bitch's lightin' a shuck!'

'Cut her down!'

'Hold your bullets, *amigos* – we have no say-so to fix her that way!'

Joshua seized the opportunity to increase their indecision. He sent two more, close-spaced shots through the front window. Conditions still didn't allow accurate use of a handgun, but they produced yells of fury from the gunnies.

His heart hammered in his chest. It was three to one. If it came to a full-scale gunfight, he'd be throwing his life away. He had to keep them occupied long enough to prevent them returning to the mounts they must have hidden in the brush, chasing the buggy and stopping Anna before she could reach town. He had two bullets left in the Peacemaker's chambers. After that, he'd have to break it open and reload.

Roache was saying, 'The damn' gal must've gotten outa the back winder. Git aroun' thar, Luis, an' we got him bracketed.'

Schwimmer boasted confidently, 'Hell, his goose is cooked already.'

Joshua thought ruefully that he was near enough right. But he had to give Anna all the precious minutes to break clean away that he could. He shouted a taunt.

'Don't count on it, boys! Biggest jackasses have the loudest brays!'

More bullets zipped through the shack's front window and door like angry hornets.

Joshua figured he was running out of options to keep their attention. Thumbing the Colt's hammer, he loosed the last of his available lead. It sped on its way, leaving him in the shack with only the smell of powder and the ringing of the shattering crashes.

God help me now, he thought.

But no power, earthly or divine, could come to his

aid. It was like a bad dream as he fumbled to reload, knowing he wouldn't do it in time.

Roache and Schwimmer had been counting his shots and took the chance he'd left one chamber empty for safety. They surged in on clumping boots and it was never clear in Joshua's mind what happened after that.

With a crooked grin Schwimmer kicked the freshly loaded Peacemaker out of his hands before he could bring it to bear.

Roache, in a blur of motion, swung a fist that took him on the jaw, hard.

He reeled, and pushed himself back up from the floor with an outstretched left arm the moment his flat palm hit the dirt.

But Schwimmer, who'd still had his gun in hand, must have turned it. Iron hit the side of Joshua's rising head. It was like a stick of dynamite went off, blurring his senses.

Apprehension dominated his last coherent thoughts. Had Anna made good her escape, or would these devils run the buggy down?

Then the gun iron got him a second time, and he fell amid a meteor shower of flashes toward a waiting landscape that was black and empty and a long, long way down.

Joshua had every reason to be apprehensive.

As Anna sent the Studebaker buggy careering back along the rough side-trail from Nate Quentin's isolated shack, she gave only a fraction of her mind to the task of driving. The rest she tried to close to the terrors of the three gun-handy crazies at her back, and the possible fate of Joshua Dillard. What if her stepfather's *brutos* caught up with her; what if she didn't make it to Ciudad del Rio, or she couldn't find sanctuary there?

She thought of the price she would be made to pay for failure. . . .

Her own panic and the crazy, breakneck pace she set for the buggy were her undoing.

The front offside wheel went into a pothole with a jarring lurch that cracked several spokes. The horse dragged the buggy out of it and they hurtled on. But with a front wheel misshapen and unbalanced, Anna had lost what imperfect control she had of the vehicle. It veered into the trailside weeds.

The disaster was sealed when the hand-forged iron rim sprang off the increasingly buckled wheel. Skilful assembly at the Studebaker factory in South Bend, Indiana, came apart in dramatic seconds on a rural road in South Texas.

The buggy tipped and Anna was catapulted from the seat. The horse pulled the wreck on for fifty yards before slowing and coming to a standstill.

Sitting in the dirt, Anna groaned. She'd broken no bones but felt the pain of bruises, frustration and fear. Her bid for safety was over. She wanted to scream out loud, but she knew it would serve no purpose except maybe to release her tightly strung nerves.

What could she do? What dare she do?

9

ANGUISH FOR ANNA

Joshua came to his senses in a grove of cottonwoods, where a light breeze rustled the leaves and whispered in the long grasses. It looked like his captors had made camp here of sorts. Evidence of a carelessly extinguished cook-fire and discarded whiskey bottles told the story. Still striving to shake off the effects of the stunning blow to his head, he became vaguely aware that one of their number, Luis Alvarez, was missing.

Kurt Schwimmer was sitting on a deadfall, building a smoke, but when he saw Joshua was conscious, he quickly put aside the makings and his hand darted to the pistol worn low on his right hip. Joshua noted his own Peacemaker was stuffed in his waistband at the left.

'The sticky beak's come around, Hank.'

Joshua raised a hand to his head and felt the tenderness there gingerly.

'What's the matter with you fellers?' he mumbled. 'Ain't these murderous shenanigans getting sort of out of hand?'

Roache's growl was accusing. 'Yuh sided that stupid, stove-up cowpoke that was Tom Hartnett's ramrod.'

'I was visiting with him. With Miss Carranza.'

'The interferin' bitch set yuh loose!'

Joshua frowned, screwing up his face as though it was a painful struggle for him to recall that.

'Your boss had no reason for holding me at the Slash C. I can tell him nothing. I've got a bad memory.'

'That ain't no never-mind now!' Schwimmer crowed. 'Grumman heered all yuh could tell an' more other places.'

Joshua said, as brightly as a man can, whose head has been rapped with the hard thirty-eight ounces of a .45, 'Obliged to know that. Guess we've got no business then and I can leave.'

But added to his myriad aches was a new one – to know whom Grumman had forced to talk, and what they'd told.

Roache didn't appreciate the sarcasm in Joshua's suggestion. 'Ain't he just the smart-aleck, Kurt?'

Schwimmer said, 'Thar's the matter of a ruckus in a graveyard and another at Mestiza's barn. Yuh grazed my arm an' it's still powerful sore. Brad Nolan got a splintered hip and Jed Parkes a broken laig.

The outfit don't take your kinda runaround from no one. Mister Grumman figures yuh owe plenty!'

'Yuh won't be goin' no place, smart-aleck – ever,' Roache said. 'When we're done, yuh'll blubber fer a bullet in the head, an' yuh'll be left as grub fer the wild varmints.'

Joshua didn't doubt their capability to realize the fate Grumman had decreed for him, but its contemplation was whisked into the background along with the blown leaves. Luis Alvarez came riding through the trees. And he led a stumbling prisoner.

Joshua's heart sank to his boots.

'I bring you the fine present we have been waiting for, *muchachos!*' Alvarez said.

He had a taut rope that had been secured with a dally around the silver-mounted horn of his *vaquero* saddle. The other end of the rope was attached to the tied wrists of Anna Carranza.

Her clothes were torn and stained. Her face was distressed and – framed in the disordered, glossy blackness of her long hair – had paled to the white of an Anglo-American girl's. But when she saw Joshua, her first words were of apology.

'I'm so sorry, Mr Dillard. A wheel smashed and the buggy was spilled and wrecked. I was unhitching the horse to ride on bareback when this – this animal seized me! He has made mad threats!'

Joshua said, 'Don't fret yourself, Anna. The rats can't kill you, too, whatever their quarrel with me.'

Schwimmer sniggered at his bold assurance.

'Nope. I allow Grumman ain't said she should die,

but she gets her needin's on account o' her high-handed interferin'.'

Joshua looked at him in disbelief. 'She gets punished for my doings?'

'Yuh didn't do to tie to, Dillard, but truth to tell, she was allus askin' to be taken down a peg with her stuck-up nose an' her sneerin' pride.'

Luis Alvarez released Anna from the lead-rope and pushed her over on to the grass. She sprawled heavily and indecorously.

Alavarez's excitement increased. Pulses beat plainly at his temples and he chuckled with devilish delight.

'We will whip you both till you are bloody and senseless, pretty *señorita,* but first we mean to have our way!'

'Yeah, why let the prize go beggin'?' Roache chirped. 'We'll take the bitch afore we slice 'em both raw with hoss whips.'

'*Madre de Dios*! No, no!' Anna cried. She was horrified to the point of hysteria. 'I am Anna Carranza! You shan't do this to me!'

'Don't care who yuh are,' Schwimmer taunted. 'Right here an' now yuh're no more'n a purty Mex filly that thinks she's somethin' special 'cos she's simon-pure. Sports can have a good time showin' a tenderfoot thar ain't a lick of sense in them tight morals!'

Joshua was angered by the treatment they had in gleeful mind for the girl. These men were Border scum of the worst stripe. With no comeback to consider, they'd abuse Anna in every vile way their lust could devise.

'That's enough!' Joshua said. 'You leave her alone now!'

Schwimmer grinned at him. 'How yuh gonna stop us? Yuh're through, Dillard – an' Carranza oughta larn thar comes a time a chili-picker ranch gal don't get to say no. She'll take it standin' up.'

'Or lyin' down!' Roache put in, smart-mouthed.

The trio had nothing at stake. Their boss, Lyte Grumman, had given them free rein. Joshua was the only witness to their depravity – and he was going to be put to death after being forced to watch the outrage.

Alvarez, overwhelmed by the prospect of turning a long-festering obsession into reality, flung himself on the girl.

'Let us see all of nature's work, *querido mio!*'

'Mercy's sake! Stop him!' Anna pleaded.

But Schwimmer and Roache stood by, laughing lewdly and feasting wolfish eyes on the full-bodied curves of young Latin loveliness uncovered by their eager *compadre.*

'Nary a *peso* for your fool honour now, Carranza!' Roache taunted.

At first, Anna didn't know what to do with her hands: to punch, to scratch or to cover herself.

'Luis Alvarez! For shame! How can you be so rude?'

All three hardcases were quickly rapt in the struggling girl's plight. And she wasn't about to give

95

in meekly to her fate. Her shrill protests and spirited yet futile resistance caused a tumult.

Alvarez cussed profanely in Spanish, but Schwimmer and Roache cheered him on.

'She is a spitfire, this Señorita Prude,' the Mexican said, 'but I swear I will soon have her like a piglet on a spit!'

Roache stood hip-cocked, his thumbs in his gunbelt, relaxed about the offence they were set to embrace.

'We're bettin' on it, Luis!'

Schwimmer watched with a glazed expression. 'An'·it'll jest be starters. Thar'll be turns. We each got cards in the game!'

Alvarez got the girl trapped under his heavy body with one hand holding her wrists above her head.

Anna gasped. 'Oh! Oh. . . ! My God—! That's enough—'

Schwimmer said, 'Not enough by a damn sight! Take a paralyzed oath on it – this ain't the half o' your comeuppance, gal. We'll larn yuh to unlimber an' go the gaits!'

'No! *Por el amor de Dios!*'

With the bunch mesmerized by the spectacle of the wicked assault on Anna, Joshua knew his one and last chance was offering. Desperate though it was, he made the only play possible. In a rush, he launched himself to his feet, lunged at Schwimmer and reached for the Peacemaker stuck in his belt.

At the last moment, Schwimmer sensed the movement and whirled back to face him.

'Keep outa this, sonofabitch!'

The barrel of the six-gun he held raked Joshua's face, drawing blood. But Joshua's reaching fingers closed around the worn and scarred black grip of his Peacemaker. He jerked the familiar weapon loose from Schwimmer's belt even as he fell away, clicking the hammer to a full cock.

Two guns roared as one.

Joshua's bullet skimmed the target, burning Schwimmer's ribs and making him screech.

Schwimmer's shot zipped over Joshua's head as he threw himself into a lateral roll.

Roache yelled, 'Blazin' hell!' and jerked into action. He hauled his pistol from its greased leather holster and fired at the rolling man.

The slug ripped into the ground alongside Joshua's head, raising a geyser of dust.

With grit stinging his eyes, Joshua completed the roll and came to his knees. He pointed his gun in Roache's direction with both hands and shot back blindly.

'Luck!' he wished himself through grating teeth. And for once it was granted.

Hank Roache was hit in the belly. He threw up his hands, dropping his weapon. His eyes widened and he gave a choked-off cry as he looked down to see blood erupting through a hole in his pants just below the belt. It was dark red and came in gushing spurts.

Meanwhile, the gunfire had arrested Alvarez's crude attentions to Anna. He looked round in shock and started to rise.

With her skirt pushed well up around her waist,

Anna's legs were free. Simultaneously with Joshua's second ringing shot, she brought up a hard, well-aimed and forceful knee into her startled molester's crotch.

'You dirty skunk!' she yelled.

Alvarez screamed like an unbearded boy at the agony of the sharp kneeing and fell on his side, doubled up.

Roache clutched the mortal, blood-pumping wound in his gut and took two directionless steps before pitching on to his face in some long weeds.

Waving his arm toward a thicker patch of the wood, Joshua shouted orders to Anna.

'I think their horses are hitched over there, among the trees. Go for them! Run!'

Joshua stormed ahead while she scrambled to her feet, trusting she would follow.

She did, but neither Schwimmer nor Alvarez were completely out of the fight. Bellowing oaths, the battered hellions sent shots that whistled frighteningly close around their escaping captives.

Anna staggered, off-balance on the uneven, root-ribbed surface. Joshua slowed and reached out a hand for her, thinking she might have twisted her ankle, but she recovered and kept on coming.

They reached the horses. Joshua unhitched all three and swiftly tightened the saddle cinches on the two that looked the likeliest runners.

'Hurry!' he said. Anna put a foot into a stirrup and he boosted her effortlessly into the saddle. He slapped the horse on the rump. It took out instantly for the road.

Alvarez and Schwimmer were crashing through the brush, cutting corners to reach the horses.

Joshua fired two closely spaced shots into the varying shades of sun-dappled greenery to deter pursuit. The trees gave him cover but made telling fire impossible, practised though he was with a six-gun.

He was rewarded with some yelling and cussing and another burst of shooting. The volley was as ineffectual as his own shots, though he realized he had to be away quickly, before they burst into sight of their quarry.

Wasting no more time on gunplay, he vaulted into the saddle of the horse he'd chosen. He lashed the spare horse into motion with the rein ends; jammed heels home to urge his own in the path of Anna's.

The horses found the trail with little guidance and they headed at a racing lick for Ciudad del Rio, hoofs drumming.

Anna swayed in her saddle.

'Slow down!' Joshua called a warning after the girl. 'We've left 'em afoot. They can't follow.'

But every yard they covered, pushing on for the town, saw Joshua more angry. He was seeing red. Nothing in his experience incensed him as considerably as the unbridled arrogance of Lyte Grumman. Plainly, he'd set his louts loose to punish not only Joshua Dillard but his own stepdaughter.

By God, it was a hell of a note.

His bitterness ran deep at the thought of the

indignities to which Anna had been subjected. As a man inclined to recklessness when fighting injustices, he swore to himself a showdown was in the offing, and this time he'd be riding to the Slash C well prepared. . . .

They were still several miles from town when Anna again swayed in the saddle.

'Careful,' he said, pulling alongside. 'You don't want to take a fall now.'

She didn't answer but set her jaw tightly and looked ahead in grim determination. Sweat beaded her brow and she looked feverish. Then, alarmingly, her eyes rolled.

Joshua leaned over and seized her horse's reins, hauling up both animals.

'What's wrong?'

Anna pitched to the ground as though in a faint.

The fall wasn't a heavy one, but Joshua jumped down with his heart in his mouth. He remembered how Anna had staggered and nearly lost her footing when they'd been running from Schwimmer and Alvarez, lead flying around them.

When he tried to lift her, his arm became soaked with something warm and sticky. Turning her, he saw the reason. She had a hole in the back of her right shoulder and blood was seeping from it copiously into the tatters of her dark blue blouse.

The puncture looked dangerously low and she was unconscious. He checked her lips.

Whether the lung had been touched, he couldn't tell, but no blood frothed on her slow breath. Yet. . . .

10

FRIGHT FOR FAITH

Faith Bloom – who'd called herself Hartnett to recruit Joshua Dillard's help in tracking the double-crossing Dick Redvers to Montana – was in San Antonio with Chet Grumman. And she was paying the price for her first stratagem's, and Joshua's, failure.

She'd swallowed her pride in turning to Chet Grumman as the second-best, if not the only remaining option. She didn't like Chet one bit. He was spoiled and mean-spirited and had only some of his father's ambition. But he had the advantages of availability, willingness and some money.

He was able and happy to buy the tickets and be her necessary escort through the expanse of the Frontier West to the wild places she had to go if she was to locate and confront Redvers; to force him to divvy up.

In San Antonio, Faith was obliged to make good

her part of the contract. Besotted though Chet was, he wasn't dumb. She'd spurned him enough in the past.

'This has to be a square deal, Faith,' he told her. 'You and Redvers cheated my father out of a valuable herd. Redvers run out on you. We find Redvers and get the money off him, what's to stop you running out on me? You being my wife makes things different, don't it?'

Too right it did, Faith thought. She could see the thoughts written on his face. Chet would never make a poker player. On the practical level, if she married him, any money they procured would be good as his – *now*, while his pa was still alive.

Chet aspired very much to be free of his father's dictatorial rule. He was also tired of his stepsister Anna, who fawned on him and threw herself at his head . . . 'yet she ain't no more fit to be a fine lady than the Mexes who run away from home to work in the parlour-houses.'

And that was a reminder to Faith it was herself whom Chet had always thought he wanted to satisfy his physical needs. She suppressed a chill shudder. His aim was purely to get both the money and the girl. . . .

But these were his weaknesses she'd played on and now the time approached for the payoff. Chet didn't intend to go further than San Antonio until she made good on part of her promise.

So at a farce of a wedding ceremony conducted partly in Latin by an alcoholic priest, Faith became

Mrs Chet Grumman, scheming all the while how she was going to put off what he plainly regarded as inevitable, bonus privileges of the arrangement.

Father Xavier received them at the side of his stone and caliche-block house on South St Mary's Street, where a purple-clothed altar had been set up in a porch decorated tawdrily with net curtains, red ribbons, candles, wild and paper flowers, and a portrait of Jesus Christ. His household staff stood in as attendants and guests.

Faith wondered if Father Xavier had, in fact, been excommunicated, but the brown-robed priest performed the rituals confidently, blessing them, joining their hands together and reciting the vows they had to exchange. Finally, he sprinkled them with holy water and gave his blessing in the name of the Holy Trinity.

'O Lord, assist this institution of marriage which You have ordained for the propagation of the human race, so that this union made here, joined by Your authority, may be preserved by Your help . . . Amen.'

Faith delicately shook from her fine silk dress droplets that seemed no less irritatingly wet than any other water, and made an extra, private vow: that she'd never bear Chet Grumman any brats . . . she wouldn't let it happen, ever.

Grinning with self-congratulation, Chet handed Father Xavier a wad of paper money and a bottle of mescal, which the priest promptly opened and tilted to his lips before offering it to the groom.

After the bottle was emptied, mostly by Father

103

Xavier, the supposedly happy couple repaired to a room booked at the renowned Menger Hotel.

Faith thought it best to establish immediately some ground rules, especially as Chet went directly to the big double-bed and threw back the spread to uncover crisp white sheets. Surely he didn't mean for them to consummate the marriage?

He gloated. 'You'll be made my woman on a bed that was maybe slept in by Robert E. Lee himself!'

Her mouth felt hot and dry.

'We must reach an understanding, Chet. We have nothing in common. Not really. This is a marriage of *convenience. . . .*'

Damn it – he was smirking at her! And the stare of his greedy, mocking eyes gave her a frightening premonition of what it would feel like to stand before him naked, waiting the taking of his pleasure.

'Sure, honey,' he said, 'but part of the convenience is I mean to claim my honeymoon, don't I?'

She tried to speak emphatically, but fear made her voice wobble. To her own ears she sounded weak.

'I-I'm not your honey. There can be no honeymoon.' Then realizing she couldn't afford to antagonize him completely while she still needed his support, she added, 'At least, not yet – not until our work concerning Dick Redvers is done.'

He sneered. 'I don't believe in that work-before-play line, Wife. And we have the honeymoon now – honey being in reference to new marriage's sweetness; the moon being the prediction of how

104

long it can last before it wanes!'

She gulped. 'Agreed. That is what they say, but we must be dignified. Can't we settle for placid companionship? We've married because our business means we must travel together. Of course, we can be friends, but only platonic—'

'You're sick, *Mrs Grumman!* – and you've gotta be cured of it, fast!'

Fright became panic. Faith turned swiftly and ran for the door. But Chet moved like a striking snake. He knocked her aside, locking the door and pocketing the key.

'Oh no you don't! No woman cheats me – least of all my wife!'

He grabbed her roughly by the arm. Twisting it, he propelled her back across the room to the wide bed.

'Let go! You're hurting me!' Faith sobbed.

His cruel fingers dug bruisingly into the soft flesh beneath the flimsy sleeve of her silk gown.

'Your sickness can be cured, Faith, but only by a strong and determined husband!'

'You're sick yourself,' she gasped. 'Control your passions, sir! Respectable women don't have need of a man. The age's best physicians say it's so. If a well-bred woman is normal mentally, her desire is small.'

'You ain't a well-bred woman. You were born in a bordello and you're a goddamn thief and liar.'

Her early life had indeed obliged Faith to be aware of the passions of what she regarded as the coarser sex. And it had left her convinced that if women were apt to be as spontaneous as men, then vulgarity

105

would destroy the polite and fashionable society she admired.

She'd also learned from observation as a child that once the young women recruits brought to her mother's former house had been seduced, their downfalls were swift and irrevocable.

'If you do anything lustful to me, I'll die!' she informed her husband.

Shaking and weak at the knees, she was nonetheless unable to stop the remorseless progress to the opened bed and the greatest sacrifice of her life.

'You and me are going to be a proper husband and wife,' Chet snarled. He turned her to face him and she smelled the mescal on his breath.

She struggled to break his hold, but he pulled her body against his own.

'Stop right n—!'

His lips descended hard and hot on hers, preventing speech. She moaned in protest, squirming and trying to turn her head. Without warning he hooked his fingers in the low-cut neck of her gown and, stepping back, ripped the bodice open.

Her fashionable corset, exaggeratedly curvaceous, was not laced but buttoned at the front. With a mighty tug, Chet popped the fastenings and she was exposed to the waist.

Faith's eyes were never more wide and vividly blue; she shrieked.

'God, no!'

She threw up her arms to cover herself, but Chet slapped her face, hard.

'Put those arms down, Faith, or I'll slap you senseless!'

Engulfed by a nightmare realization of her physical weakness, she did as she was told.

He thrust her backwards and she fell into the accommodating softness of the big bed's mattress. It seemed to absorb resistance. She steeled herself for the worst.

Despite her prediction, Faith didn't, of course, die. But over the following days she remained implacably hostile to meeting Chet Grumman's repeated marital demands, making a bigger travesty of her vows than the drunken priest's dubious ceremony.

She was also filled with self-loathing by what she survived; left with what felt like nausea at work in her vitals. Chet told her she must respond to the instinct of nature and that she would 'soon be up to her business as a good wife'.

No, she didn't die . . . but she made a further vow – that once Chet had served his purpose, and she safely had her share of what had been taken from his father in the rigged poker game, he would.

And whether or not he killed Dick Redvers.

Doctor Ashley Roscoe had practised in Ciudad del Rio for a dozen or more years. Joshua knew the whereabouts of his house and surgery, a large old frame building down a street off the plaza. The house boasted a second storey and around eight rooms. Out back, in the cool shade of a huge mariposa tree, was an adobe outbuilding that served discreetly as the town's mortuary.

Anna Carranza, who hadn't properly regained consciousness, was alive but maybe only just. Joshua hadn't wasted a moment, knowing none could be spared. She'd groaned when he'd picked her up and briefly her eyes had flickered open. He'd lifted her into the saddle of his commandeered horse and climbed up behind her. Holding the reins in one hand and wrapping his free arm around her slim waist, they'd ridden double this way, completing the journey to town at a walk. Even a mild canter had made the near-senseless Anna moan complaint and furrow her brow in pain.

Joshua guided the horse to the hitch-rail outside Doc Roscoe's surgery. His arrival was noted and he didn't need to go in to summon help.

Ash Roscoe himself came out of the house.

'That gal isn't dead, is she?'

'Bullet wound,' Joshua replied succinctly. 'The slug was nigh on spent when it hit her and it's still in her shoulder. Her breathing's worrisome shallow. . . .'

Roscoe tutted. 'Gentle! We'll ease her off and carry her into the examination room . . . the bullet will have to come out.' He adjusted steel-framed spectacles. 'Why, it's Miss Carranza!'

Ash Roscoe was pushing fifty. He had thinning, iron-grey hair on his head, but a showy, straggle-ended moustache. He had been a Union surgeon during the War. Since then – coming south to find a new niche as a physician – he had competently set broken bones, delivered babies and prescribed cures for fevers.

They put Anna, bloodied and limp, on a cushioned, sheet-draped table in a room that smelled vaguely of carbolic. Roscoe did some more tutting when he saw how her clothes had been ripped. He checked her pulse, detecting the slight beat.

'These Mex gals! Always getting into trouble . . . but Anna Carranza!'

He shook his head; Joshua offered no explanations. He preferred for the moment to let the medico go about his work.

'Oh, yeah, I can get bullets out,' he rambled as he prepared his instruments. 'I got a heap of practice both in the War, then in this neck of the woods when young Anna's step-pa was meeting opposition to his expansion ambitions from Tom Hartnett and the like. The big problem in all the Border country is the Mexes who go to the *curanderos* first and proper physicians last.'

Joshua knew of what he spoke. In the past, in Texas and other South-western places, he'd had his own quarrels with the Mexican section of the populace. It had a tendency to call in orthodox medical aid last – after injuries or ills been subjected to the attention of old crones whose traditional remedies could involve the disembowelling of

109

chickens or yucca root poultices. Sometimes the *curanderos* dressed wounds with mud and herbs, virtually guaranteeing infection.

In Anna's case, Joshua had used a clean, folded part of his torn shirt to make a compress to staunch the flow of blood and brought her promptly for the doc's attention.

Roscoe uncovered the wound. The puncture was small with very little ragged flesh around its puckered edges.

'I don't think any of the bleeding is internal. Like you said, the bullet was spent and it's lodged against the bone, but the patient has lost blood and her body is in shock. The danger with major blood loss is that the body's vital organs shut down and the patient proceeds into death. You did well to stem the bleeding. What she needs now is rest – rest aplenty.'

After coaxing a little laudanum-based tincture between Anna's lips 'to prolong insensibility to pain', Roscoe wanted to work quickly. Joshua held down the patient's shoulders to keep her immobile and watched anxiously as the doc probed sensitively with long, sharp-pointed forceps which he'd sterilized in the open flame of a lamp with its chimney removed.

Anna uttered a groan in her coma. Roscoe frowned, then skilfully gripped and withdrew a chunk of lead he dropped into a small steel bowl.

The wound was bleeding again. He bathed and irrigated it with a disinfectant solution in a pan. The solution quickly became reddish, but the doc had the cleaned hole re-padded and bandaged in moments.

The glint in the eyes behind his specs might have been humour or cynicism.

'Well!' he said, washing his hands. 'That's two women with gunshot wounds I've seen in a matter of days. Most uncommon.'

In a strange way, Joshua knew he was about to hear something that would startle him.

'Oh?' he said.

'Yeah, the other unfortunate lady probably died the instant she was shot. . . . Thankfully, I figure a more successful outcome can be predicted in Miss Carranza's case, though I fear she's growing a mite feverish.'

'What happened in the first case?'

'That was a mystery. Shot point-blank in the heart. Mind, she also had additional, less explicable injuries. Reckon how it was, her former profession could have earned her enemies – old grudges, old motives for loosening a tongue, then stilling it.'

'So tell me, who was this other woman?'

'She was a retired brothel madam. Her name was Belle Bloom.'

11

JOSHUA GOES CALLING

The town's mortuary, conveniently shaded by the ancient and massive mariposa tree back of Doc Roscoe's house, was known as the 'cool shed' but it was more an adobe hut. Its thick walls were whitewashed in and out and the floor was tiled.

Large, neatly labelled pharmacy bottles were arranged on a shelf in soldierly ranks – arsenic solution, formaldehyde and chemicals Joshua hadn't heard of.

And what he smelled here wasn't carbolic but the indescribable smell of death.

'The deceased has a daughter,' Roscoe told him. 'But she seems to have left town and no one knows when she might return.' He lowered his voice ominously. 'If she ever does in circumstances that are plumb queer.'

The doc pulled back a sheet over a corpse laid out on a marble-topped table.

In death, Belle Bloom was even more gross than in life. But Joshua's eyes were immediately drawn by one particular.

'Good God! The soles of her feet are covered in burns – bad burns.'

Roscoe nodded solemnly. 'It would appear to have happened shortly before she was shot.'

Joshua made a closer inspection of the woman's corpse.

'And her fingernails – several mashed, like the fingers have been squeezed between the jaws of nutcrackers or suchlike!'

'That would fit the injuries.'

'Is the law looking into this?'

Roscoe hunched his shoulders. 'Such as the law is in this county it looks the other way when something like this comes up. It never moves without certain parties' orders anyhow.'

'Do all the good citizens accept this situation?'

A ghost of a flush came into Roscoe's face.

'Folks who admire to stay in business hereabouts are minded to accept it,' he said stiffly.

Joshua didn't express his exasperation. What had he stumbled upon in this place?

He summarized in his head what he thought he'd learned about Lyte Grumman, his stepdaughter Anna, his son Chet and the Blooms, Faith and Belle. He also made some suppositions that produced explanations of sorts.

113

What puzzled him most was the mystery of the murder of Belle Bloom.

What had been the motive? What purpose had her shooting achieved?

By Anna's telling, backed by Nate Quentin's evidence, Faith had joined up with Chet Grumman and lit out in pursuit of Dick Redvers who'd headed north weeks since with ill-gotten gains.

Lyte Grumman had earlier been ignorant of, or blind to, the falling-out of the card-room tricksters, Faith and Redvers; also that Faith had failed to profit from the stolen herd.

Later, Grumman had made clear to Joshua that anybody who hitched up with Faith, on whatever terms, was asking for trouble. The irony seemed to be that his own son had done this very thing and quit home and the Slash C, presumably to help Faith complete the same mission for which she'd tried abortively to enlist Joshua.

Joshua's assumption was that Lyte Grumman had found Belle Bloom's hideout home in the hollow. He remembered how Kurt Schwimmer had crowed how Grumman had heard all he wanted someplace else. Maybe that was from Belle Bloom, and maybe the 'all' was little more than what Anna had guessed – that Grumman's Chet had teamed up with her Faith.

Which brought him back to the puzzle of why Belle had been shot dead. If she'd talked or not, killing her served no purpose. She could accuse Grumman of having her beaten – tortured in point of fact – to make her speak, but where could she lay

114

charges? Law in Ciudad del Rio was sewn up in favour of the Grumman faction, as Ash Roscoe had just confirmed.

He said aloud, 'Maybe I should return to the Slash C and have this out with Lyte Grumman.'

Roscoe shook his head wonderingly. 'You are a very – brave man, Mr Dillard.'

Joshua knew it had been on the tip of his tongue to say 'foolish'.

'Grumman's gunnies are apt to shoot the hell out of an unfriendly *hombre* who strays on to their graze,' Roscoe went on.

'Yeah, and maybe they won't,' Joshua said. 'Time is ripe for a parley and I mean to have it, is all.'

'Study on it,' the doc advised. 'Though all power to you, I guess.'

Joshua put the broader issues aside to arrange for the care of Anna Carranza.

'I'll have a bed prepared for her in a back room upstairs,' Roscoe said. 'She can stay privately till she has recovered, though that might be a matter of weeks rather than days.'

Joshua thanked him, although he had a suspicion the promise was secured by his expenditure of more of the money that Anna had retrieved for him from her stepfather's cash box. The Bennett gift wouldn't last forever, but Joshua felt that Anna had earned a portion of it.

Warily, he returned to his room at the hotel, where he planned to sleep on the problem of his next planned moves and whether he should reconsider them, heeding Ash Roscoe's warnings.

He had an obsessive hatred of injustice and the ruthless lawbreakers who took advantage of the rawness of frontier communities to ride rough-shod over the innocent. It had become ever more deeply ingrained in the long years since he'd been made a widower by the killing of his wife in San Antonio. His recklessness and high-handed methods had cost him his job with the Pinkerton Detective Agency.

Operating privately, his gun had been for hire when the dinero was right and the assignment took his fancy. Exasperatingly, experience had taught him first and foremost that his policy was no trail to riches. Invariably, he was at the bottom of barrel financially.

Now a cautious medico was advising him to turn his back on a mess into which he'd been tipped by a sentimental journey to Texas. Was he getting soft to suppose that, having for once a little money on hand, he could consider the advice?

His code asserted itself. When the next morning's light cut slim shafts into his room through the cracks around the window blinds, he awoke with his anger rekindled.

A grudge had to be avenged; if you didn't assert your rights, they were lost forever to those who were bolder. Justice must be done the Dillard way, taking the law into his own hands as the occasion called – damn the cost and the consequences!

His harsh treatment by Lyte Grumman could not be brushed aside and forgotten. Daringly, he decided to stick with his intention to force a showdown with the arrogant cattleman – face to face, one on one.

Maybe it was pride that drove him against the impossible odds of Grumman's pack of gun wolves, and maybe it was beyond the ken of a right-thinking person, but he was determined he would bring the man to account or die in the attempt.

On the edge of what was by use if nothing else regarded as the Grumman acres, a pineboard sign had been hammered on to the wide trunk of an old cottonwood at a fork in the road. Stamped lettering read:

THE SLASH C
No entry except on business
Trespassers shot on sight
By order of Lyte Grumman, Owner

'Hmm!' Joshua mused to himself. 'Well, I guess this ride is on account of business.'

He rode a dusty trail for an hour, encountering no one. He did distantly glimpse a team of *vaqueros* driving about thirty head of milling cattle in a direction they didn't want to go. Though obscured by a broad dust cloud, the critters looked like scrawny culls and the Mexes working them, he suspected, were the hands who did the real ranch work of the Slash C. They were not Grumman's hired gunfighter types. Nevertheless, he rode more cautiously less the *vaqueros*, spotting him, should take the unlikely course of shooting him 'on sight'.

Eventually, the Slash C's fortress-like headquarters came into view, with its walled compound, the outbuildings that flanked the big house to either side and the corrals out back.

Joshua noticed that the massive wooden gates that opened on to the courtyard were closed.

The place looked prepared for a siege, except for another pair of Mexicans working lackadaisically on replacing a broken corral-pole.

Grumman was probably aware Anna Carranza and he, Joshua Dillard, had escaped his wolves. Was he expecting reprisals from a disgusted town, feeling guilty at last about its tolerance of his high-handed ways?

What would be Grumman's own next move?

Joshua maintained his guard. Suspicious of what might prove a trap, he turned his horse from the trail. The country was rolling plains, but on the uplands, Texas grama and other grasses gave way to several types of oak and to denser mesquites and junipers. He rode into the woodland of a low ridge from where he could observe the ranch house.

Joshua reasoned his best plan of action was to wait till nightfall before he advanced on the stronghold, in the hope of catching the boss – Lyte Grumman himself – unawares. Preferably alone. . . .

The afternoon hours slipped by. Nothing much happened except normal ranch activity. The sun sank in the western sky, painting the landscape mingled hues of gold and purple. Men, most of whom wore Mexican sombreros, returned to the headquarters. None was recognizable as a Grumman hired gun with whom Joshua had tangled.

While he watched from the darkening shade of the trees, Joshua cleaned and oiled his Peacemaker. He filled the loops in his gunbelt with cartridges.

When it was dark, he checked that his horse was securely hitched to a stout oak. He drank the last of the water from the canteen he had brought along and, the familiar Colt in hand, glided from his cover and moved toward the black bulk of the *hacienda*.

He crouched low as he could beneath the sides of a shallow gully and kept the woods in which he'd hidden at his back. He realized how easy it would be to skyline himself inadvertently against the last vestiges of the sundown's orange glow.

Joshua reached the compound's wall without challenge and crouched in its shadow. His ears were alert for the sound of human approach, but all he heard was the incessant chirp of cicadas and other night sounds, near and far.

Holstering the Peacemaker, he moved carefully along the wall till he came to a section where the adobe had been broken and crumbling repairs made. His vision had adjusted to the dark by now and he used the imperfections in the wall to scale it gingerly, then swiftly roll over and drop into the soft dust on the yard side.

A cool wind had blown up, chilling the sweat on his brow.

Voices were suddenly raised in the bunkhouse,

speaking rapidly in Spanish, but it was some private argument and no one ventured out into the yard.

In a half-dozen, catlike bounds Joshua crossed the open space to the house, where he ducked behind one of the flower tubs on the front gallery. Heady perfume – was it honeysuckle? – filled his nose but nothing worse happened and he successfully stifled an urge to sneeze.

Joshua worked his way along the house front in the deep shadows of the covered gallery. By dint of expert feel, he finally located a window that was improperly secured and eased up the lower sash.

The house was as quiet within as it was outside. Joshua began to fear that the place was indeed shut up, unoccupied by its master ... in fact, totally empty.

He was in a tiled hallway in near complete darkness. He could swear no lamps were in use anywhere in the house. He dared to strike a match. It showed him bright Mexican rugs scattered on the floor, the unlit oil lamps in a glass chandelier overhead and a curved stairway to the upper level.

An open door to a parlour showed only more furnishings that were a mixture of Anglo-American and Mexican styles. But he hadn't come to appreciate the grandeur or even to snoop.

'Damn!' he murmured. 'The bird's flown and time's wasting.'

He gave brief consideration to a search of the empty house, but discarded the option. He didn't think it likely to produce any firmer pointer to his prime interest – Grumman's present whereabouts – than his best guesses. Of Grumman's background and activities, he'd heard report aplenty.

He picked his way in the dark back to the window where he'd forced entry.

He was back on the front gallery, passing the last of the tubs of flowering shrubs, when a bulky Mexican stepped out from the corner of the house, barring his way.

'*Pardon, señor,*' the Mexican said with exaggerated politeness. 'Mr Grumman is not at home, and you will not find him climbing in and out the windows. For this, *el patrón* would expect me to shoot you. . . .'

He raised his right hand and grasped the wrist with his left.

Joshua found himself looking down the barrel of an old but very menacing Orbea Hermanos revolver modelled on a Smith & Wesson .44 and originally of Spanish naval issue.

He heard the click as the hammer of the revolver was thumbed back. His stomach muscles crawled, tightened.

12

GAMBLING IN BUTTE

'Listen to me!' Joshua rapped urgently. 'What d'you owe Grumman? Your boss's stepdaughter, Anna Carranza, a clean-living girl of your own race, has been attacked and shot by Grumman's dogs. She's at the doc's house in town. She could be dying. Did you know that?'

He knew instantly that his intuition had allowed him to play successfully on the weak spot in the Slash C set-up, which was Grumman's reliance on lowly paid Mex and mixed-race hands to do the ranch chores while highly paid, mainly Anglo gunhawks pursued his ambition of rangeland domination.

The one group was basically honest, maybe sometimes unwilling, even lazy, but with pride, honour and morals. The other was arrogant and amoral. The tension was evident in the Mexican's faltering response.

'But you break into *el casa.* . . .'

Joshua nodded firmly. 'So for this you'll murder me? Before you shoot you should think about the consequences. And about Anna, who has been raped.'

The Mexican's swarthy face creased in a frown. He was faced with dilemma, uncertainty. The moment of indecision was all Joshua required. Before his hold could tighten again on the wavering Orbea, Joshua dived for his legs.

The Mexican's pistol went off with a flash of flame and a roar, the bullet whistling harmlessly over his head. The pair crashed to the boards of the gallery, up against a heavy flower tub filled with regularly watered dirt. Joshua wasn't slow in following up what he knew would be only the momentary advantage of surprise attack.

He grabbed the Mexican's ears in both hands and smashed his head hard against the solid earthenware tub. The man's eyes rolled and his senses fluttered and vanished like the flame of a blown lamp.

Joshua leaped to his feet, leaving the heavy body crumpled up against the tub. Potential investigation of the unexplained shot in the night threatened. He had to move fast or there'd be a passel of the *hombre*'s fellow ranch-hands swarming all over him.

Throwing caution to the winds, he sprinted for a magnolia tree growing close to the compound's perimeter wall. The tree went up thirty feet and retained many of its lower limbs unpruned.

Joshua shinned up it, finding plenty of hand- and footholds. He pushed his way through the glossy leaves, knocking off several of the big and fragrant, creamy-white flowers, and came into a fairly dense but rounded crown, which partly overhung the wall.

He dropped on to the top of the wall. From there, he lowered himself on the outside to the full stretch of his arms and dropped as lightly as possible to the ground.

It was some fall. His ankles were jarred, but fortunately they weren't broken or sprained. He was able to make a swift dash for the wood that had been his afternoon vantage point and where he'd left the horse.

It had not been a profitable expedition.

On the hell-for-leather ride back to Ciudad del Rio, he did some serious thinking.

Lyte Grumman had evidently succeeded in forcing Belle Bloom to divulge knowledge that Joshua figured had sent him and his gang of ruffians off on the tracks of Grumman's son, Chet, and Faith Bloom.

Joshua could no longer escape the truth that Faith was a smart but disturbed woman and he'd been caught badly in the sticky web she'd woven. She'd been a damned good liar, no less. And if he was peeved about falling for her lies, he also had to confess to a cold fury about the beatings he'd suffered on the orders of Lyte Grumman, the blood that had been spilled – which included the slaying of the informant Nate Quentin – and the fact that his best helper, Ann Carranza, was hovering between life and death.

He determined to see through to a just conclusion the appalling misadventure his journey south had become.

Montana called ... it was a distant and big territory, but it was an old stamping ground where Joshua had worked in his Pinkerton days and had later briefly served as a town marshal. He still had contacts and friends. He'd use them to bring this bitterly unsatisfactory affair to a finish.

'Till death us do part, Faith!' Chet Grumman said to his icily beautiful new wife. And the sarcasm was plain.

He was persisting in extracting maximum pleasure from what he was pleased to call their honeymoon, overruling Faith's objections in the latest of a succession of hotel rooms.

'You're sick,' Faith said with a shudder.

'I never said I was perfect.'

It was the closest he came to apology.

The pair's travels had brought them to Montana by way of Salt Lake City and the Utah Northern Railroad. The line had been extended to the boomtown of Butte after three and a half years' work financed by the far-seeing 'robber baron' Jay Gould. Business magnates and Wall Street speculators knew an electrical age was coming. This made copper the new gold ... and Butte had rich copper deposits.

Faith and Chet found Butte thriving with an influx

of newcomers other than themselves. Immigrants from far countries – China, Cornwall, Wales, Ireland, Germany, Sweden, Finland – flocked to work the mines' vast, high-grade veins of copper sulphides that stood at steep angles and ran fabulously thick thousands of feet deep and long. Others came, as they always had, to supply or exploit the needs of the miners.

In due course, it was in this likely place that they ran Faith's former ally, Dick Redvers, to earth. He was working as a dealer in a gambling hall in an alley off Wyoming Street, not far from their hotel. The district was one where a man could find everything he might want, from whiskey to women, plus gambling, which had been the great American pastime since the earliest years of the century.

Dressed for an evening of polite sport, Faith and Chet went to observe Redvers at the tables and layouts of Pop McGuigan's Dance and Gambling Hall. If the chance offered, they would confront him about the money he'd collected in San Antonio from the sale of Lyte Grumman's cattle.

Faith meant to have her share; Chet meant to continue proving everything that was hers was his.

'We'll start by asking him a few simple questions,' Chet said.

At Pop McGuigan's a sign over the wide, panelled door said, 'A dozen faro tables round the clock.' It was a large, newish building with a prosperous, respectable brick front. In fact, the whole structure was brick since the Butte city council had passed a law requiring all new uptown buildings to be of brick or stone after a disastrous fire had destroyed the bustling central business district in 1879, the same year Butte had been incorporated as a city.

Inside, Faith and Chet sat on stools at the elegant rosewood bar and ordered drinks from a bartender in a spotless white shirt and black bow tie. A piano-player was tapping the keys in a far corner, but though hostesses in formal gowns circulated the room and were doubtlessly available as partners, no one was dancing.

The chief occupations were drinking, faro, poker, twenty-one, monte, dice and roulette. Besides its ornate bar, the imposing main chamber had a huge back-bar mirror, several life-size paintings of nudes, and heavy, red velvet curtains and hangings. The gilt and glitter was lit by brilliant chandeliers.

Dick Redvers was spelling one of his fellow house men at the dice table. He looked every inch his part. He wore a white linen shirt, black string tie, a fancy flowered vest and dark striped pants; a neat, dark-haired man with an indoor complexion and clean-shaven but for a pencil moustache.

Faith had to smile ruefully at her optimism when she thought of how she'd tried to kid the hapless Joshua Dillard this man might have played a key part in driving a thousand head of unpredictable, wicked-horned, longhorn cattle from Texas to Montana. Seeing Dick again, the very notion became ludicrous. Even had she gotten the gallant fast gun to lead her to Montana and her quarry, he would have smelled a rat.

Redvers was tossing dice and fading bets for the house. Five players were at the table, taking turns with the dice. When one of them quit, Chet took his place.

Redvers paled visibly.

Faith felt she was in sight of her triumph at long last.

Chet spoke quietly into Redvers' ear. Redvers looked over, saw Faith and was startled. His face turned from fish-belly white to pink. He shook his head.

But Chet had a run of apparent luck and by the time the regular dice-board man returned from his rest, he'd doubled and re-doubled his ten dollars' stake money. He scooped up the pot and stuffed it into his pockets. Then, when he quit the table, Redvers came with him to the bar and Faith as though in tow.

'Faith!' he said, trying to put on a bold face. 'What is this? From what Chet Grumman tells me, congratulations are in order!'

Close up, he was as sartorially flashy as ever, with a familiar favourite ring, set with a big diamond, on his right hand.

Faith stared him down.

'My status calls for no congratulations, if you must know, Dick Redvers. It's changed only because you cheated me! I was left with no money and I needed a man to help me come find you, you stinking welsher!'

Redvers attempted his best poker face, but it

wasn't working for him.

'Look here, that herd money wasn't anything like we'd bargained for, Faith. I had expenses—'

'Sure . . . some on account of running out with my share – of hitting the long trail! Chet intends to see I collect the debt, Dick, so you'd do best to think about coming across pronto with a big hunk of dinero.'

Redvers shook his head sadly and spread his hands.

'Faith! Faith! There is no money. It's all gone. I lost the lot playing the tables, I swear. Why do you think I'm working here as a house man?'

Chet Grumman growled, 'He could be right, Faith. Hell, these tinhorns are always in and out of luck, specially when they cheat and get called.'

'As I say, I've nothing to offer you just now except my congratulations. And now I really have to get back to work, or Pop McGuigan'll be fixing to fire me.'

Chet said, 'Well, we'll be around a while and waiting, Redvers.'

They could scarcely put Redvers under physical restraint with the gambling hall's burly bouncers looking on from a discreet distance. He left them.

Faith was hugely frustrated. She knew Redvers as only an ex-partner in duplicity could. She always knew when he was lying.

As she seethed, Chet muttered to her that they had to play their hand coolly. She was agreeably surprised when he showed initiative by calling over the spotless bartender, drawing him into conversation, and tricking him into divulging details of where Dick Redvers was living.

'Yep, like you saw,' Chet assured the white-shirt, 'Dick is an old pal of ours. We'd like to deliver him a gift unexpected – brung all the way from San Antone.'

The servile barkeep was amenable to helping a thoughtful patron and impressing his handsome woman.

'He's got hisself a cabin on Butte's outskirts, in the shadow of Big Butte, the volcanic cone to the north-west that gave the city its name.'

Directions delivered, they thanked him and departed.

'A pleasant walk on a cool evening, sir, madam,' the bartender murmured, pocketing the silver dollars they left on the counter.

Chet said, in the street outside, 'We'll get the Redvers snake alone, Faith. I've a hunch I can get him to sing a diff'rent song.'

Faith figured he was right. She knew how little backbone Dick Redvers had when it came to a fight.

13

PAINFUL PAYOFF

The cabin rented by Dick Redvers was situated on a rough sidetrail. It was a bleak, secluded plot. Though the lights of the city were still brightly visible, Faith and Chet were reliant on the full moon for the expedition they embarked upon after returning to the hotel to change into more suitable dress.

'We'll be waiting for him when his shift ends and he comes home,' Chet said as they looked the place over.

The cabin was a simple two-roomed shack of rough-hewn timbers crying out for creosote or pitch. Not much showed through the windows, though the furnishings they could see were appropriate to convenient bachelor quarters, chosen for low cost, privacy and as a place of retreat and sleep.

At the back, Chet broke a window pane, got in and came to the front to let Faith in through the door.

The place was musty with the shut-up smells of old

cook-fires, tobacco smoke and unwashed clothing. A saucer on the table was full of cigarette butts. They lit no lamps but sat in darkness, till Chet ran out of patience and started turning the place over, dumping the contents of drawers and cupboards on the floor, cutting open a mattress.

'Settle down, why don't you?' Faith said, coming to the back room's door. 'You can't see what you're doing anyway, and I doubt he's stashed his loot anywhere so obvious.'

Chet replaced the mattress on the cot and threw the bedding back on top. He leered. 'Maybe we should pass the time on his blankets.'

It was getting along to dawn when they heard the crunch of approaching footsteps.

'He's here!' Faith hissed.

Chet flattened himself against the wall alongside the closed door. When the homecoming card-cheat opened the door and lurched in wearily, Chet stepped out to hit him, and hit him hard. He knocked him down with a paralysing uppercut.

Faith gasped, but her eyes glittered and her lips smiled in malicious satisfaction. She'd waited a long time for this moment.

Redvers shuffled backwards across the floor on his backside, groaning. He raised a hand to his bruised jaw and pulled himself up by the table.

'What is this? Get the hell outa here!'

Chet's lips drew back in a snarl.

'We said we'd be around. You owe us plenty. This is payoff time, if'n it means busting your goddamn neck!'

132

Faith said, 'Give us what we want and you won't get hurt.'

As Chet advanced on him, fists clenched, Redvers raised a hand.

'Lay off me! This is stupid. I vow and declare I haven't a red cent to my name!'

Faith scoffed and pointed to the showy diamond ring on his finger.

'Oh, yes, I can believe that! What about the ring?'

'That's mine! I've always had it. You know that, Faith. But here – you can have it. Just don't hit me again! Go away!'

'Go away!' Faith mocked. 'I think not. I know you, Dick. The very fact you can offer to give up your prized ring tells me you have other money – maybe a large percentage of the Grumman herd money – hidden away safely.'

Chet grabbed him by the collar and slapped his face from side to side.

'Tell us where it is, rat, or you'll find out we're real bad medicine!'

Redvers blubbered, 'I can't! I can't!'

'Can't what?' Chet said. And punched him repeatedly in the belly, doubling him up breathless, helpless. He collapsed, sobbing.

Faith said, 'We're wasting time. The idiot won't see sense till we start to inflict real damage. What properly scares you men is always the same. . . .'

She pulled down a clothesline strung across the low rafters. 'Hogtie him, and I'll find a sharp carving knife. I know how to do it. My ma never found out, but as a kid I watched her work on a dirty bucko who was one of a pack of *bandidos* that had abducted a parlour girl. Ma's burly menservants held him down. When the foul creature figured his state as an entire man was under threat, he cried like a baby and spilled everything he knew.'

She searched the room with emotionless eyes. 'I'll also need a suitable lamp without its chimney – to heat the blade in the flame.'

'You d-daren't, Faith Bloom!' Redvers stuttered.

Chet grinned evilly. 'Hell, ain't you a piece of work when it comes to hating men, Mrs Grumman! It sure won't pay ever to turn my back, but for now I figure you got an idea that's plumb salty.'

Redvers went to pieces when Chet trussed him up, popped the buttons on the carefully tailored striped pants, and got him on his back across the solid, pineboard table, having swept off the saucer with its remnants of old smokes. Drops of perspiration stood on his pallid brow.

'No, no! Not that!' he whimpered, his face a mask of fear. 'Mercy!'

Distastefully, without batting an eyelid, Faith nicked him with the point of the big knife, producing a glistening red bead of blood.

'Talk, damn you!'

Redvers uttered a choking, sobbing sound.

Chet winced and shivered, though the atmosphere was closer than ever in the cabin.

'You can't do this!' Redvers managed to blurt.

'She is doing it,' Chet said. 'You want to remain

134

unaltered, it's time to say just what you did with the cattle money.'

Faith said nothing, but with a steady hand returned the knife to the lamp flame. And then she applied it again, turning it so the flat of the blade made contact. The burningly hot surface singed hair and flesh.

A faint smell lifted, like a scrap of meat might make when it was dropped accidentally into a cook-fire.

Redvers' hips bucked and he screamed shrilly like an animal caught in a trap. He gave in. His surrender tumbled out in a gasping, gagging stream.

'Stop! Stop!' he pleaded. 'I'll tell you where it is – where I buried the stuff!'

And Faith laughed without humour, a savagely exultant sound in contrast to his pained anguish.

'This is what we want to hear. Keep talking, Dick Redvers, or the consequences of a quick cut will be irreversible. . . .'

'Let's have it, Redvers,' Chet said. 'If'n you ain't convincing, she'll start on you again, an' this time I 'spect she'll slice 'em right off. Faith don't cotton to *cojones* nohow.'

Joshua Dillard enjoyed an atypical stroke of luck directly on his arrival in Butte, Montana.

He'd come to the city as a result of a tip-off from old connections he'd wired at Pinkerton's National Detective Agency headquarters in Chicago. 'We never sleep' was the Pinks' motto, and Dick Redvers, a suspected crooked gambler with a record in the agency's famously innovative files, had been spotted in the wide-open copper-mining centre. Butte was attractively full of hundreds of saloons and gambling halls and their sucker patrons. It was no great surprise that Redvers should have gravitated there.

But the first people Joshua saw and recognized in Butte were none other than Faith Bloom and Chet Grumman!

He froze and drew back into the arched porch of the railroad depot. Other disembarked train passengers flowed past him on to the street. Several business types, some Eastern and foreign, evidently expected buggies and carriages to be conventionally waiting for hire outside the station.

This wasn't the case. Only one buggy was left and an argument was developing over who should have it – a drummer from the arrived train, lugging a sizeable sample case, or Faith and Chet, who'd approached from the opposite direction.

Joshua retreated into the waiting-room and found an observation point beside the front window. After a deal of wrangling and gesticulation, the row ended with the drummer, apparently outbid, stamping off angrily behind an urchin who'd been summoned to carry his baggage.

Interestingly, Faith now took an active part in negotiations. She wheedled charmingly and the dickering led to the handing over to the buggy driver of a further wad of greenbacks. Then Chet Grumman climbed on to the buggy seat and took up the reins of the two-horse team. The driver handed up Faith.

Interesting. . . . It appeared the pair had successfully solicited to rent the conveyance on a self-drive basis.

Joshua cussed quietly. It looked like he was going to lose the pair as quickly and fatefully as he'd found them. Emerging from the busy waiting-room, he stormed past the windows of the ticket-office and out on to the street.

But the buggy was gone.

Joshua found himself in a strange town he'd last visited years back when it was little more than a bunch of mining camps. He was in what was now a moderately crowded, major city of the West: new buildings, new businesses, new people in a community that looked like it must be mushrooming literally by the day. Butte had passed quickly through her days of gold and silver. Joshua had read someplace that its mines had produced 5,000 tons of copper in a single year. In these parts, the Copper Kings' enterprises were outstripping even Montana's enormous range livestock industry – and the fabulous profits in cattle were well known to have attracted investors from England and Scotland as well as the East.

Joshua sensed a familiar air of optimism and boosterism.

But what was he to do now?

In towns, detecting was in large percentage foot and mouth work. You walked places; you asked questions. So that was what Joshua did. He traipsed the brick-lined streets and alleys, fuming over Faith and Chet's departure on seemingly urgent business in a buggy. With the benefit of the Pinkerton details on Dick Redvers, he came to his known place of employment, Pop McGuigan's Dance and Gambling Hall, within a half-hour.

The co-operative bartender in the bright white shirt and bow tie said, 'Another friend of Mr Redvers?'

Joshua asked more questions of his own, discreetly but purposefully stacking a pile of coins in front of him. The coins gradually made their way across the bartop, into the 'keeper's pocket. Joshua soon had the whole story of the two other friends who'd planned to surprise Dick Redvers, though he took many of the hints made to be the emanations of an overheated brain.

'I guess they made a night of it. Dick don't live in no rooming-house but kinda private,' the loose-tongued barkeep disclosed in hushed tones of confidence, 'an' he ain't showed up for work this morning. The lady – uh – that is, the *couple* sure was mighty han'some folks.'

Joshua, too, was given the directions to Redvers' cabin and informed it was an easy walk. He decided not to head there on foot, however. Faith and Chet Grumman had needed wheels for some reason, and he had a shrewd notion that, whatever he found at Redvers' place, he might require better transport than two legs himself.

He also reckoned matters were moving fast to a showdown and hoped his intervention wouldn't be too late to prevent more killing. . . .

He had his own motives for sorting out this sorry business, which was assuming more and more the character of a mad wild-goose chase. It was still coming home to him how much of a cat's paw he'd become, nearly taking on Faith Bloom's dirty work for her. But now she had a new pawn: Chet Grumman was her dupe. Or was she his?

Joshua was beginning to wonder where his true sympathies were best placed – that was, apart from with Anna Carranza, languishing in an unknown state of health in a small Texas town south of San Antonio.

He went to a side-street livery barn, of which Butte had several, and rented a saddle mount, a calico mare.

The ride to Redvers' dwelling, just outside the city limits, took only minutes, and there the hunch he'd played was confirmed.

The rough track to the cabin traversed a drainage ditch. In the mud at its bottom were the distinct and fresh impressions of two sets of wheels, one deeper than the other.

Joshua frowned and looked more closely. He quickly figured the ruts had, in fact, been made by the same vehicle, despite their slightly different appearance.

He read it that just a single visiting rig had carried a heavier load on one of its passings through the ditch. And the implication to be drawn from all the circumstances was that Faith and Chet had come calling on Dick Redvers again – today – in their hired buggy, and that this time they'd been accompanied by him when they'd driven back out.

Joshua moved on to the cabin itself, noting where recently horses had been allowed to stand and more wheel tracks had turned in the dust. He found the cabin's door locked, but he also discovered the broken window back of the property and used it to gain entry.

The evidence of a rude search of the place was clear. The contents of open drawers and cabinets were spilled on the floor and, in the bedroom, handfuls of stuffing from a cut mattress were strewn around.

Back in the kitchen area, he came upon a yet more ominous find. Beside a wreck pan, but left unwashed, was a vicious looking carving knife. It had congealing blood on its tip, which had attracted a feasting fly.

Small spots of what looked like the same blood were on a table top, toward the edge, and on the floor beneath. All the spattered droplets were still sticky.

Heading out under the front door were skid-marks that could have been made by heels being dragged across the floor.

A chill knot formed in Joshua's belly.

He didn't think the ransacked cabin would tell him more. It was time to put his tracking skills to a bigger test – and to ride in pursuit as hotly as the tracking allowed.

Would it be fast enough?

14

NO WORK FOR
A LADY

The buggy wended west around hills and through
wooded vales. Dick Redvers, tied hand and foot,
showed them the trail to take.

Faith knew he wouldn't try to double-cross them.
Not now. He'd accepted she and Chet Grumman –
herself particularly – weren't playing. They meant
business.

He complained at first that the abused anatomy
where she'd applied the point and the heated blade
of the kitchen knife gave him acute pain with every
jolt of the buggy.

'Shuddup!' Chet said.

'Sorry . . . I'm in pain something fierce, I tell you,
like it's still on fire. She shouldn't've done that. I can
scarce think which way to go.'

Faith leaned across and grabbed the buggy whip
off Chet. She prodded their defenceless victim with

the rounded, blunt end.

'We'll stand no stalling!'

At Redvers' wail of torment, Chet chuckled. 'You'd better guide us right, dumbhead! Your ex-partner's a mean an' ornery lady!'

And gratified by Redvers' distress, Faith poked again, stirring a bit and causing him to squeal and squirm.

'Quit whining, Dick. I let you off lightly. After that *bandido* told my mother where his pards had hidden the stolen dove, she carried on and cut him anyhow.'

She'd often dreamed of wreaking similar vengeance on vulgar manhood, but she'd never thought the dream could be brought about. How vulnerable and puny Dick Redvers had been back at his cabin! He was a no-good who'd cheated her. How satisfying it had been to have the fate of a man in her hands! The power and control had been all hers.

Then again, she'd already paid Chet Grumman an unagreed, extra price for his assistance in hunting down Redvers and making the pleasure possible.

Perhaps it was as well that Joshua Dillard had failed her. She didn't think he would have countenanced the torture of Dick Redvers. Nor, though, would he have raped her. The first occasion, in San Antonio, Chet had so exhausted her with his ruinous lunges that she'd fainted clean away. . . .

Chet didn't know it, but the time would come for him to pay, and more dearly than Dick Redvers.

'How much further is this place, Redvers?' Chet asked.

They were following roughly the course of Silver Bow Creek, downstream from Butte. Years earlier, this had been the first hive of the district's mining activity.

Redvers said, 'I hid the money way out of town in the old gold diggings, beside one of the abandoned prospectors' hovels. No one goes to those places any more.'

During the gold mining spell in the 1860s, the main action had been seven miles west of Butte. Thousands of prospectors had toiled along the banks of Silver Bow Creek and its gulches.

Water hadn't been plentiful and the placer men had met huge setbacks. Often, they'd tried to haul gravel down to the creek for washing with rockers and sluices. The landscape had been ravaged of timber and torn up with excavations in attempts to build long ditches and flumes to bring the water to the diggings.

The operations had proved too costly, too difficult. Silver Bow City, a collection of rough and unattractive camps, was now all but forgotten. The gold and the silver years had passed; copper promised to make Butte historic and unique, attracting investors from Salt Lake City, New York and Boston.

Dick Redvers directed his captors into the scarred ugliness of the desolate Silver Bow country. His chosen trail led through a narrow cut with pine-stumped slopes on either side.

Abruptly the pass opened on to a ridge

overlooking a gulch. The bare ground below was dotted with heaps of tailings, ragged diggings and a scattering of broken-down log shacks with flat sod roofs long fallen in.

'This is the place,' Redvers said. His tone was flat; demoralized. 'The cache is buried where the disturbance don't attract any attention – an old hole that was dug plenty before, behind the last of them cabins. The money's there, stored deep and safe for hard times.'

'Better damn well be there,' Chet growled.

They rode down.

Chet reined up and he and Faith climbed from the braked buggy back of a ramshackled miner's hut. Chet staked the horses and dragged Redvers off the seat. He drew a pistol and cut the prisoner's ropes.

'Get the spade we brought, Faith,' he said. 'This shouldn't take long.'

Faith balked. 'Digging isn't women's work.'

'Nor's gelding.' Then he laughed harshly. 'Naw . . . no digging for you. A wife's duty don't lie thataway. You ain't left Redvers any too frisky, but he's still got arms that's sound, never mind his hands are soft as a woman's. He'll dig!'

Faith fetched the spade and flung it down at Redvers' feet. He bent over painfully to pick it up. At Chet's gunpoint, he shuffled toward a distinctively misshapen rock.

'I left it right here,' he grunted. Sweat already on his brow, he levered the rock aside.

'Start digging, damn you!'

145

Redvers began turning out the crumbling dirt that had been immediately under the rock.

'Hurry it up!' Chet snapped, waving the gun. 'You might have blisters someplace else, but there ain't none yet on your mitts.'

Redvers leaned into the job, every shovelful of dirt seeming to make him gasp and grimace as waves of pain spread from the aggravated, burning soreness in his groin.

Steadily, the pile of excavated dirt grew till he stood knee-deep in what looked like part of an old ditch.

'You better not be fooling, tinhorn,' Chet warned.

Faith felt irritability returning. She'd been forced to endure weeks of her own punishment – from Chet – and this was not her natural setting, standing around amidst filth and squalor.

As soon as the money was retrieved, she determined to make her much anticipated bid for her freedom. She'd wait no longer. Dick Redvers was cowed and impotent; Chet was the danger. What she had to do was dispose of him promptly once his purpose was served.

And that moment was rapidly approaching.

Irritability transformed into anxiety. She feared strength might fail her – not mental strength, for she was capable of anything in her new condition, but physical strength.

Chet said, 'Goddamn it, Redvers, you trying to sink a mine shaft?'

Panting, Redvers struck again with the spade, and

the sharp, heavy blade thunked into something of more solid texture than the friable soil. He paused, pale and dripping with sweat.

Chet swore and the edge in his voice was scornful and threatening.

'What now? What kinda bluff are you running?'

'It's the tarp I wrapped round the satchel . . . the job's about done.'

Redvers scraped dirt away, to reveal the buried bundle.

He threw aside the spade, wiped the back of his hand across his brow and stooped to unearth the recovered treasure with his bare hands.

The knowledge that the loot from the biggest coup in Redvers's cheating life was at last about to become his caused Chet to put aside his caution. Fearing nothing from the broken-spirited and fatigued card player, he holstered his gun and pushed him out of the way.

Redvers staggered and fell, starting to sob again, piteously.

Chet ignored him. He dropped to one knee in the dug hole, tugging at the tarp, eager to get his hands on the prize.

He pulled out the leather satchel, already stained with grey mould. Rising to his feet in the excavation, he shook it on high by the handle, laughing victoriously.

'By God, it's mine! All mine!'

None of them noticed a drum of approaching hoofs as three riders emerged, skylined on the rim of the gulch's far side, and paused.

Abruptly – possessed by ice-cold determination – Faith made her move.

She picked up the heavy, discarded spade in both her hands and took tight hold of the shaft. She made a mighty, two-handed swing with it and was thrown completely off her feet by the uncontrollable momentum the tool's weight generated.

She yelled wildly.

But by then it didn't matter. The spade's sharp edge had hurtled full-tilt into her husband's conveniently low neck, nigh on decapitating him.

The half-rotten satchel spun from his grip, splitting open. Gold coins and green bank bills arced through the still air mingled in a spray of red like the disintegrating parts of a grotesque rainbow.

Chet Grumman was felled in a sprawl on his back in the dirt, eyes wide and sightless. His head was at an unnatural angle and bright blood spilled from the jagged wound that had half-severed his neck.

Faith picked herself up at the same moment as Dick Redvers.

Redvers, seeing that Chet was deader than mutton, dived for the six-gun at his belt and yanked it loose.

Faith, armed only with a bloody spade, thought he was going to shoot her dead in retaliation for what she'd done to him, and to recover the ill-gotten, stolen Grumman fortune he'd always fixed to enjoy alone. But he swung the gun up in an opposite direction and yelled.

'Lyte Grumman an' his hardcase gunnies! They followed you, you stupid bitch!'

Her gaze swivelled.

Three horsemen were charging down on them with what looked like murderous intent, guns drawn. She recognized them all with awful, heart-lurching shock.

As Redvers said, it was her arch-enemy, Chet's father – boss of the Ciudad del Rio country she'd fled not a month past – along with two of his most ruthless killers, Kurt Schwimmer and Luis Alvarez.

And she could scarcely doubt he must have just seen her strike dead his son. The wrath of God couldn't be feared worse.

Nothing else for it, she bolted like a rabbit for the dubious shelter of the tumbledown shack. Her prime objective was to get inside, bar the door. Maybe if she could lie flat on the floor she'd escape the bullets sure to fly.

But her zig-zag run was calculated to pass the split satchel. She dipped, seized the still bulging bag and swept in as much of the spilled money as she was able.

It was an act of split-seconds. Then she hurried on, clasping the blood-spattered harvest to her bosom.

15

THE SECRET STORY

Joshua Dillard's task was not an easy one. Painstakingly, he made out the tracks of the buggy leading from Dick Redvers' ransacked cabin.

Through brush, trees and pastures he went, looking for tell-tale signs. He observed the ruts in undisturbed dust and through the occasional soft patches, usually low, where seeps from underground courses had dampened the surface.

In harder places, he noted the stones with tiny marks on them where horseshoes had chipped and scraped. In overgrown places, he read the message in trodden-down and run-down stems of broken grasses. Through a timbered stretch, he mentally registered twigs with white ends where growth had impinged on the little-used trail and recently been snapped off.

When the surface was arid and hard, Joshua had to dismount more than once and cast around, but ultimately the tracking was brought to a premature end before he came in sight of the rig.

A brief volley of gunfire crackled someplace ahead in the wasteland of the old Silver Bow goldfields.

Joshua put the calico mare into a run and rode straight for the sounds. He reasoned straight off that gunplay in the now sparsely populated area was likely mixed in with the business he was following.

He was mindful that Lyte Grumman and his inner bunch of gunmen had left Texas shortly before him. Though he hadn't had time yet to enquire into their whereabouts since arriving in Montana, the odds were that their quarry was the same as his and that they were ahead of him.

He came to the head of a cut and was at once on a commanding ridge. It overlooked a raw and unsightly gulch littered with the debris of bygone gold prospecting. Three men on horseback circled a corpse sprawled on its back in some diggings. Even from a distance, Joshua had no doubt it was a corpse from its lack of motion and the spreading quantity of blood darkening the dirt beneath the twisted head.

He could also put a name to each of the riders: Lyte Grumman, Kurt Schwimmer and Luis Alvarez.

Grumman turned to the sod-roofed hovel close by.

'Come out with your hands in the air, Dick Redvers!' he hollered. 'You're a damned cattle thief an' we'll give you a fair trial as one!'

Joshua figured the offered trial would be informal,

held in no court but promptly in the open air. And it would end with a hanging from the nearest tree.

Redvers, who was apparently cornered in the shack, figured the same.

'Never! You can't shoot – there's a woman in here. Clear off!'

Luis Alvarez laughed. 'You make jokes, *amigo!* You are sheltering a sick temptress and murderer. Mister Grumman is very upset!'

Intent on impressing the boss, he dug spurs into his horse and stormed the hovel, emptying his gun into its walls and the spaces that were its windows.

'Careful, Alvarez!' Grumman ordered.

No one fired back immediately, but as the foolhardy Alvarez wheeled his horse to gallop away, Redvers emerged from the door and threw a brace of shots.

Alvarez stopped one of the bullets with an audible smack that knocked dust from his dirty white shirt, front and back. He screamed and threw up his arms, then toppled over the rump of his mount in a backwards somersault. His heels cartwheeled, the silver-inlaid, large-rowelled Mexican spurs flashing.

His body struck the ground with a solid thump.

Schwimmer recovered fastest. He hauled a rifle from his saddle boot where he sat his horse by the first dead man – whom Joshua surmised to be Chet Grumman. He whipped the long gun to his shoulder, squinted down the barrel and slung a hard shot into Redvers from a safe distance.

Redvers dropped Chet's six-gun, throwing open

152

his arms with a sharp, shocked cry. A splotch of crimson showed where he was hit mortally in the chest. He promptly fell over backwards, lifeless.

Three men dead!

One girl left at the tender mercies of a bunch of gunnies!

Grumman bellowed, 'Faith Bloom! I've more men back in the rocks, you poor gal! You're cornered, finished. Bring out my money and give up! There's nothing else you can do.'

His arrival unnoticed by any of the participants, Joshua decided it was time to take an active part in the grim drama. He sent the calico sliding pell-mell downslope, rubble spurting from under her hoofs.

'Hold hard, Lyte Grumman!' he roared, pulling to a standstill in a cloud of dust. 'Any more shooting will be on equal terms. Your men'll not riddle an unarmed woman with bullets, you dirty bastard!'

Grumman recovered quickly from his surprise. He sneered. 'The fast gun! How gallant! It's *she* who's the bastard!'

Joshua rapped, 'Get down and fight like a man! We'll have this out, one to one . . . in a fair duel!'

'Fool talk!' Grumman said, starting to look a mite pinched and white.

'I say you're yellow as a canary bird, Grumman!'

'Damn you, mister, no man braces me and lives!'

Though an inveterate bully, Grumman had a fierce pride and he swung down from his saddle.

'This is loco, boss,' Schwimmer said, still stunned by the unexpected loss of Luis Alvarez. 'You don't

153

have to go ahead with what he says.'

'Naw, I can accommodate him if that's what the sticky-beak wants.'

Joshua slid from his saddle. 'I do! We'll play this square.'

Grumman's sneer deepened. 'I say your number's up, Dillard! Follering to Montana is your big mistake. You don't know what you've ridden into.'

'I'm waiting, Grumman!'

The cattleman was lightning fast; faster than Joshua ever expected. Joshua thumbed the hammer of his worn Peacemaker, thinking with sick alarm that he'd lost.

The blur of action was unreal; the shots were as one. The swiftness of two flaming Colts merged in one ear-battering blast.

But Grumman was a split-second too hasty and his aim awry. The breath of hot lead whistled past Joshua's left ear.

Joshua, more measured and steady, scored a hit that broke Grumman's gun arm. His gun span from his nerveless hand and his other came up to clutch the wound.

Gunsmoke swirled around them.

Joshua stood steady as a rock, his feet solid and slightly apart on the ground, long legs braced; the smoking Peacemaker held ready. He turned his bleak gaze on Schwimmer and said, 'You're owed for your part in what happened to Anna Carranza. You're welcome to the same chance.'

It was a tense moment as their eyes locked.

Consequently, they both missed the movement behind them until it was too late. So did Grumman occupied by his painfully shattered arm.

Faith darted out from the leaning, bullet-riddled hovel. And she carried a weapon. It was a miner's old five-pound hammer with an eighteen-inch hickory handle, dark with age and rot.

She made little sound till she was right up to Grumman. Then she swung the hammer with the same double-handed action she'd used with the spade that had felled Chet.

The first sound was the dull thud as it smashed Grumman's skull; the second was her shrill, manic laugh.

Grumman fell instantly, but the hammer rose and fell repeatedly till the deteriorated handle broke across its grain and the piece with the forged steel head hurtled off, dripping blood and brains.

'God Almighty!' Joshua said.

It was too late to save Grumman; it took help from Schwimmer for Joshua to hold and subdue the unhinged woman.

'We're friends!' Joshua said, but they had to work hard to convince her of it.

Finally, they got the stump of the bloody hammer away from her and quietened her some. She lapsed into an uncontrollable, breathless shivering, though the temperature was warm.

Joshua thanked Schwimmer but warned, 'Any tricks from you or any pards nearby and you're through.'

Schwimmer said, 'Grumman's dead. We've had a bellyful, Dillard. We ain't askin' fer no more trouble.'

'Fine,' Joshua said. 'I think the poor woman's over her fit, but nothing's going to be easy.'

Faith clutched at him; clung to him desperately. She made wild, whimpering sounds in the back of her throat.

'Wash off the blood! The men must be stopped and I must be pure again. The woman who yields to man's passion and loses her virtue is a prostitute. I have acted to redeem myself! I must be pure!'

Surprisingly, Kurt Schwimmer had a key part to play in the final explanations.

Joshua got to the bottom of it in Butte after Faith had been placed in the care of the city's law. She was declared by the doctors who examined her to be mentally unfit to face criminal charges. She was cowed and terrified. Frequently, she'd be frozen with fear, though she seemed to understand Joshua had been returned to her as her helper.

Joshua said to Schwimmer, 'Grumman got his needings. If she hadn't killed him, he would've been liable to kill her out of hand – just like the mad dog did the mother after she'd told him what he wanted to know and pointed him in the direction of his son and Faith.'

'Nope,' Schwimmer said. 'Grumman wouldn't've thrown down on Faith. You've got it wrong.'

'I have?'

'Damn' sure. He weren't goin' to do it on account

156

of it would've been gunnin' his own flesh an' blood.'

'I don't understand what you're saying.'

''Peared Faith Bloom was his brat as well as Belle Bloom's.'

Joshua could scarce believe his ears.

'What! You're telling me Faith Bloom was a half-sister to Chet?'

Schwimmer nodded solemnly. ''Xactly. The mad bitch married her half-brother an' has kilt him an' her own pa, though I guess she's all unknowin'.'

'Explain!'

With a lift of his shoulders, Schwimmer carried on.

'Sure. Lyte Grumman did kill Belle Bloom, like yuh say, but it weren't to silence her or jest fer the hell of it – it were a sorta provocation. The ol' madam had opined it great retaliation fer her cruel treatment to let the ol' man know Faith'd bin taken fer a wife by his son an' heir!'

'I don't believe it!' Joshua exclaimed.

'It's what happened. Ol' Belle was plenty tough. After he made her say where they'd gone by burnin' her feet an' mashin' her fingers, she got back – tauntin' him with the claim Faith was his daughter well as hers. Seemed he sowed the seed one time in the Ciudad del Rio brothel she'd run.

'Grumman denied it, but she kept on with her story, goading him an' shamin' him in front of his men. Finally, the knowin' – an' the knowin' we knew – made Grumman snap. He shot the gross cow point-blank in a plain fit of fury.'

Joshua took long moments to digest the

astonishing revelations. Somehow, it did fit perfectly with what he'd already known of the story of the young woman raised in a brothel, ignorant of her full parentage, despising men. She'd been aloof, full of vanity and poise. Made herself a damned good liar. Now she was a sad shell, her mind destroyed.

For Joshua, the unsolicited case and its denouement confirmed once again that there was more to justice than you read in a law book.

Also once again, it was a misadventure that left him no profit, though he still had charge of the money Dick Redvers and Faith had taken from Grumman in the form of a herd won in a crooked card game in a room above the Black Jack Saloon in Ciudad del Rio.

He set some aside in the care of a respected Butte attorney to fund Faith's continuing care in an asylum.

Then he returned south to Texas, toting the rest.

Anna Carranza was in a rocking chair on the porch of Dr Ashley Roscoe's house.

She was surprised and pleased to see Joshua Dillard again. He was looking tired but happy.

'How are you?' he asked. 'Recovering?'

'Slowly. The doctor says I'll be all right. It will always haunt me, of course, but well – that'll fade in time. Soon, I must find a new home. I can't dare go back to the Slash C and Lyte Grumman. There's no place for me there any more.'

Joshua smiled, even happier, it seemed. And he

went on to tell her the most incredible story.

He finished, 'So you see, you're not only free from the tyranny of a brutal stepfather – the whole spread is yours. In effect, Grumman stole your land out from under you, legally. I checked the position with attorneys and top men in the land offices of the Department of the Interior. The Slash C was your birth father's property before his widow remarried Lyte Grumman. With Grumman and his son both dead, the best information is that the deeds to the ranch will return to your name.'

Anna was overwhelmed by the news. Once it had sunk in, she realized that she had a huge responsibility with the reassignment of the Slash C to herself, the sole survivor of the Carranza family.

'Mr Dillard, you must become the manager of my estate. I owe you so much.'

Joshua laughed and shook his head.

'I don't think I have the makings of a good *mayordomo,* or even a bad *vaquero!*'

'Then you must have what's left of this money that was taken from the ranch by Dick Redvers and Faith Bloom with their crooked card game.'

'No, Anna,' Joshua insisted, 'that's the Slash C's and every cent will be needed to hire reliable workers and restore its ravaged fortunes as a decent livestock operation.'

Standing, Joshua thrust out a hand to shake hers and put his other on her shoulder.

'So long, Anna, I hope the scars soon heal. All the scars.'

He went out and swung into the saddle of the horse he'd arrived on from San Antonio. She lifted a hand in final farewell as he turned the mount's head north.

Within moments, he'd cantered out of her sight and out of her life, around a curve in the street.

Anna sighed. He'd explained he was some kind of undercover troubleshooter and that he was well accustomed to the money he made or saved going not to himself but to others. She didn't think that could give him much of a life.

Nor was it very fair. He'd deserved more reward than mere thanks. A lot more.